WAYWARD SUNS

HAMELIN BIRD

PIPER HOUSE

ISBN: 978-1-7354891-6-2 (paperback)

WAYWARD
SUNS

I:BLOOD BROTHERS

Spike was dead at the back of the bar. His joints were stiff, rotted through and still throbbing, his body cold and damp. He was singing.

He didn't seem dead—not really—and no one seemed to notice his sore body off to one side; some pointed, plenty laughed, but most carried on as if he just wasn't there, tired faces sweeping the room before gargling their Quaaludes with Heineken. Almost all would've sworn he was alive, even the ones who wanted him dead; they'd point to the smoke pouring from his mouth and push coke mirrors to his nose and take turns wringing out his face. Yet even more would claim he was *truly living*, getting the very most out of life, perhaps for the first time all night. But even as the beer pulsed through his body, attracting horseflies and making his pores sweat, as the barroom started to kind of sway and with Richard Pryor on TV, Spike's heart was cooling and numbed over like a lump of raw meat left on some February doorstep.

This was back in '87, a few months after that fella from West Germany flew his plane—a Cessna 172, I believe—straight through Soviet air defenses and landed in Red Square. Around that time, anyway—same year Baby Jessica fell down that well over in Texas. Before O.J. and the L.A. riots and the World Wide Web. Everything was different back then—witnessed through a *brighter lens*, let's say, a kaleidoscope of colors that are no longer around— and sitting up nights, occasionally I wonder what I wouldn't do for that one-way ticket back to glory.

I was standing down near the wet rooms, watching Buster shuck oysters from behind his slimy wooden counter. I liked to watch his hands dance around the shells, splitting them effortlessly, the way he worked the blade and the little rivers of light that streamed down the glove when it was wet. Then I looked closer and noticed the sign dangling behind Buster's head, the paper stained a pale shade of yellow:

Consumer Advisory
Eating raw oysters, clams, or mussels may cause
severe illness. People with the following conditions

*are at especially high risk: liver disease, alcohol-
ism, diabetes, cancer, stomach or blood disorder, or
weakened immune system.*

And then it said:

*Ask your doctor if you are unsure of your risk.
If you eat shellfish and become sick, see a doctor
immediately!*

More than the freshest catch of oysters and
clams, however, more than the promising ebb of
domestic and imported and draft, of weekend spe-
cials and Duplin wines, by far the most popular
tonic served at Ernul's was the *power to forget*. Served
alongside this most alluring of aphrodisiacs came
the pinnacle of pride: the offer to be sacred, one
night at a time. This was the true ambrosia. And if
it wasn't your night, if things just didn't add up and
you were tempted to say they never would, then
you always reserved the right to embarrass yourself and, in the morning, say, "I didn't know it."

I moved across the bar, dodging wide-mouthed
heads flung back with laughter and about a thousand chips nestled squarely on the shoulders of
a gang of drunken loggers. Spike sat sipping his
beer at our usual booth, a battered old wraparound
from which we watched the crowds come and go;
on late nights they'd start to bob and weave, and
sometimes they would dance in their seats, and if
you looked just right some claimed you'd see them

fading in and out of existence and then—*poof!*—they'd up and disappear...but I'd never seen anything like that.

I was young then.

Only some nights when it was late and the bar was gutted, and empty bottles lay scattered like Stonehenge across the table, a song would drift from the speakers—John Cougar maybe, or CCR—and Spike's eyes grew foggy beyond their lenses. His soul sank low, and slamming air drums or plucking at strings that just weren't there, he was the closest thing I'd ever seen to anyone *actually* dipping out of existence; he was all of our own black holes of repressed memory: deep, for sure, but so deep you could never touch bottom, never get a good look through the breathless, impenetrable dark.

He turned now as I settled into the booth, his tattered ball cap resting majestically next to him on the table, and not missing a beat I tossed on a grin and ran a couple fingers through my long greasy hair.

"*Ey mon! whadda priddy boy like ya doan in a place like dis? Lost? Ya starvin', mon?*"

Spike hacked out a cough and turned away.

"*What da matter? Tell me, mon! Sing me ya troubles!*"

"C'mon, Wes..."

"Fine, all right," I said, dropping the accent. "Haven't seen you around last couple days, neither has Prentice. Didn't know if we'd lost you for good this time..."

"Been working," he told me. "Worked all last weekend and every day since, twelve days straight, and I'm about *this far* from puttin' my boot right upside Kevin Hillebrandt's head." He lit the last of his smokes, slammed down the lighter. "Man don't do nothing but *whine*, Wes, and anything else he does it backwards."

At the time Spike was doing construction with one of the local crews, hard labor that relied on the weather and meant long hours boiling in the sun. But really Spike's home was the sea, working the trawlers out of Fairfield Harbor—and a slew of ports beyond—though recently he'd had trouble finding a spot on any of the boats. Occasionally some of those Fairfield guys dropped in to hork oysters, and although they slapped Spike on the back and made all sorts of promises about getting him a gig on the boats, I knew really they hated him and made fun of him because of his glasses and called him *Spic* when he wasn't around to hear it.

"I'm just *tired*, Wes, and gotta be up at five tomorrow morning to fix everything the Genius messed up today. Sounds fun, huh?"

"What about Saturday?"

"And?"

"You available?"

"Now I'm not workin' the weekend," he snapped. "I don't care, I'll *quit* before I work the weekend—Kevin Hillebrandt can kiss my royal ass." Spike jerked his cigarette over the tray, breathed smoke at the tacky lamp dangling overhead. "Wouldn't mind if I borrowed a couple those, bud, till I get paid tomorrow?"

I slid four Marlboros across the table, and filing them into his empty pack Spike paused suddenly and, not looking up, said, "So...he's playing tomorrow, right?"

"He's playing, all right," I told him, scoping out the rest of the bar. Thursdays were fantastic bar nights, the last chance at a little peace before the weekend started, without the hustle of strangers and fair-weather freaks. "If he ain't dead, he's playing."

"I missed the show last weekend, meant to go..." Spike's voice trailed off, slipping away as he stared absently at the cherry of his half-smoked cigarette. "We'll hafta catch it this time."

After a few more rounds Spike stood and slipped into his hat, stretching as he made ready for the long walk home. I offered to cover the booze and, after a few requisite denials, he let me. Then he was gone, taking with him any real interest I had in being there, so finally I swallowed the bit of suds at the bottom of my bottle and stepped outside, stumbling from the bar and farther along the trash-guttered streets toward Prentice...

§

Not long before I'd moved to Reelsboro, one of the local stations—Channel 9, I think it was—did this whole story on my cousin and his band. They interviewed Prentice and showed him on stage, screeching into a microphone or pounding his guitar. Then they'd cut to the audience, and they had to blur out about a thousand different things because there was this couple near about making whoopee in one corner, and a fight in the other, and sometimes there'd be this little blur in the back of Prentice's *head* when he turned it just right. My father said you could practically smell the smoke through the TV screen.

The band was Olympus, and after the story aired touring musicians from all over the state started dropping in to jam with them. And although theirs was definitely a hard rock act, they were heavy the way Zeppelin was heavy—generally blues-smitten but something of a slut style-wise, with a few out-of-place "Tangarene"s and "Kashmir"s and the occasional ten-minute drum solo— and they'd had all sorts sit in with them. Oh, they'd had jazz combos and *a cappellas* and saxophones and cellos, and once even this *interpretive dance* lady. I'm not kidding, the entire show she stood stage left doing this freaky technicolor mime routine dressed in a leotard and dark sunglasses.

Thing is, the kind of music they played, you didn't hear a lot of that back then. Not on the radio, at least; as far as rock went, this was the heyday of hair metal and androgyny and Spandex ballads. Alas, among the casualties were portent glimmers of hope, evidences of the rougher edge of rock to come: thrash metal had just come shredding out of the closet, the virtuoso rock heralded by Eddie Van Halen was in full swing, and in only a few short years the grunge invasion would tear out of Seattle, finally twisting the knife on everything that came before. And if things were different and all this would've never happened, you'd no doubt have seen Olympus right up there with the big boys, scribbling on tits and losing Grammys to Jethro Tull. But you wouldn't have caught them so much as breaking static back in those days, 'cause they didn't manufacture that kind of glam metal aerial manure.

Finally the pavement turned to gravel under my feet and I came to the Yard, a withered mire of bones and mud cast in the shadow of a certain mountain that, farther along, loomed up sharply from the earth. Small enough, not postcard material but pretty in its own way, and come tomorrow night half of Reelsboro County would flock here like lemmings and set up for the show, curling on quilts beneath the stars and whispering dreamily about the songs and how they seemed to vibrate from somewhere deep inside the mountain itself.

The sky burned pink along the horizon as I started the long journey through the pines, following the twisted path to my cousin's. His place wasn't much, really just this old barn Prentice claims he stumbled over back in middle school, says he used to sneak girls up there to get wasted and pork; Prentice also once told me he'd murdered his mailman and buried him under the porch. We were *ten*.

I'd caught the first glow of candlelight through the trees when a sudden breeze swept past and with it Prentice's voice, creepy in its sing-song cadence and haunted by a drum and lulling bass line. Moments later the barn loomed into view, the words WELCOME TO THE PLEIADES scrawled across the front in fluorescent neon paint.

The tune was "Gravestone Excalibur" and the band was still hammering it out when I walked through the door. As always, the place was layered in candles, a thousand burning eyes in the darkness, and by their light I spotted Neil and Johnny Remarks at a desk in the corner, laughing and playing cards—Johnny was losing—over a bottle of gin, and this guy Slick down on his stomach behind a couch. Couple girls dozing up near the stage, beer cans scattered around. And there, perched on a makeshift stage across the room, I saw Prentice strumming wildly at his guitar, crooning through squinted eyes as Bob jostled the bass and Rick slapped a sturdy, well-worn beat on the drums.

I started over, shuffling through the darkness and past long-abandoned quilts and couches and oddly-placed ottomans. No beds, however, and there was a running joke around town as to when Prentice actually *slept*—and whispers, not entirely untrue, that he didn't. I'd grabbed a book from one of the shelves and was flipping its pages when a sudden squeal split the night—an anguished, raspy cry of something like loneliness that set the girls twisting in their sleep; Neil and Johnny dropped their cards and were turned, daydreaming off toward the stage.

Moments later the yowl faltered and finally fell off, and in its pin-drop absence I tapped a cig from my pack of smokes, then sparked the end and pulled down a drag, blew it out. Then it was my voice that filled the room.

"Show us your boobs!"

Prentice turned, his face veiled darkly beyond the curtain of his wavy black hair. Quick as a whip, he dropped his guitar and sprang from the stage, the cigarette tossed from my lips as he snagged me in a headlock and gave it a grind.

"Let up, man! I said fucking quit!"

"Make me," he grunted, was busy serving another grind when I squirmed out and landed a quick kung-fu kick to his ass. But Prentice only laughed, waving for the band to take five as he led me to the nearest cooler, popped the top and tossed me a cold one from inside. His pupils were huge.

"Listen," he said, "you might wanna watch out for Lil' Dee..." He bent forward, lighting his cigarette from a candle. "Dude's been north and fuckin' south last coupla hours...benzos, I think, must be comin' down." He gave me a wired look and said, *"Careful Wes, there could be blood..."*

I glanced over, saw Lil' Dee down on his stomach near the stage, wallowing in some kind of puddle of something. Sloppy bastard.

"Good to know," I told him. "Dropped by Ernul's earlier, saw guess who?"

"Oh?" He looked amused. "And what'd he hafta say?"

"Not much. Worn out, same as always."

Prentice popped his beer, slurping down half in a noisy gulp. He asked if Spike was still with Kevin Hillebrandt, and when I told him he was Prentice made a gagging noise and said, "You ask me, Spike just needs to go ahead and kill that rat, get it over with. He coming this weekend?"

"He said he was, but...I don't know what Spike's gonna do."

Prentice burped. "Neither does he, I think. You best be here too, slack."

"I'll be here," I said, holding up my hands.

"Oh, I know you will. 'Cause if you're not I'm gonna find you and jam a garden hoe up your doo-dy chute. Here, take this. A little something to hold ya over..." As if by magic, Prentice made a baggie appear out of his pocket, stuffed it in my hand.

"No," I said, turning it back. "I don't—"

He pushed it away.

"Take it, Wes."

"But I don't—"

"Take it Wes,"—*whispering*—"before Lil' Dee comes over, tries to shank my ass with a tooth-brush."

I scoped out the bag—promising—then slipped it into my pocket. "You don't have to do that, y'know? I don't need your charity."

"Well, tell me who does?"

"Apparently Lil' Dee does."

"You're right, so shut up. Now sit down. Get high."

Prentice tossed away his smoke, frogging me hard in the shoulder and then hopping back on stage before I could return the favor. A couple weeks earlier the drummer, this guy Rick, he'd clipped a big oak on his three-wheeler and nastied up one of his hands. I asked him how it was holding up and Rick answered with a fast run on the drums, which left me pretty much stranded. I mean, how're you expected to respond to something like that? It's not like I carried around a little set of tom-toms so I could hammer out a few beats of my own whenever I asked somebody how their wrist was holding up and they just spanked their drum. So I just kind of smiled like an idiot and said "ah" loud enough that only I could hear it. Then I grabbed a seat in one of the empty recliners.

"*All right!*" Prentice gulped the last of his beer and then launched it through a window, snatched up his acoustic and gave it a bang. "*Let's do this!*"

The music swam down in waves, washing over me as I leaned back and closed my eyes, dreaming of the slow dance of candles and the burning constellation they'd left in my mind. Then only the music remained—just the music, nothing else mattered—and when it was over I opened my eyes and caught sunlight arcing through the windows, the only sounds those of the old chandelier creaking back and forth over the stage, rocked by an early morning breeze.

The place was deserted.

Only the junior misses remained, still tangled

in a mess of sheets near the stage. Newbies, mostly, though one *did* look a lot like one of Rick's old flames, a sweet girl who almost always had sucker and lollipop poles sticking from the sides of her mouth. Prentice couldn't have gone far, probably fetching all the gas we'd yanked late Tuesday night; it was past four in the morning by the time we'd lugged back the jugs, stashing them in the old poplar grove between—

"They went to the store."

I sat up, turning in time to catch a thin twig of a girl with pretty blue eyes appearing from behind the stage. She clicked her tongue and said, "You just missed them, sorry," and my eyes zeroed in, studying devilish shorts and a cute belly shirt showing off a tight tummy and dark Caribbean tan. She seemed familiar, somehow, and for a moment I was sure I'd met this girl somewhere before...

"Let me guess, they were up all night? Again?"

Her face went blah. "He's *your* cousin, you know they were. This will be their...third night, I believe? Wait!" She flinched, waited, gave up. "Oh, who can keep up anyway?"

"Are you with them?" I asked. The band, I meant. Groupies.

The girl tittered, maybe offended. "No, I'm not with the *band*. My girl Kat, she is, but...I don't belong to anybody." She started over, her sun-polished legs glowing like soft fire as she ran fingers through her streaky blonde hair. "I've seen you around, y'know. Don't think I've ever heard you say more than four words, though. But you *do* talk if you're in the mood, I know that much."

"And how do you know that?" I asked, playing up my suave bank robber gaze, part Clint Eastwood but mostly De Niro.

"Prentice told me."

She smirked at me, and was moving closer around an ottoman when suddenly I saw her problem: she used too much make-up. Not *way* too much, but it was a tad overboard, enough to make me realize she probably had a real problem with mirrors and self-worth...or that she came from a circus background.

Still, there was something about this girl that made me sweat, it's like I couldn't think straight. She was definitely hot in that sleazy Miss October spank-fest sort of way, but I could see her going Drama Queen in about two seconds flat.

Thanks, but no thanks.

"Well, look, do me a favor will ya? When they get back, tell Prentice I'll catch up later tonight."

She took another step. Now I could feel her breath.

"They only went to grab some booze and some other things for tonight. You don't have to leave so soon, y'know." She started picking at the button of my jeans, right above the zipper, and rubbing at my belt. "Please don't go," she said. "The other girls are sleeping and I've been up for an hour now...I'm *bored...*"

Her hand crept down the front of my pants.

Oh boy.

Still, much as I would've liked nothing more than to take this girl to a discreet corner and lay down some serious roadwork...something in me simply wouldn't budge. I tried imagining myself talking to her, I really did, but for some reason it always came out sounding like Porky Pig on crack.

Fingers, gently caressing my crotch.

And then I remembered Prentice's show later that night, when the beer would be cold and plenteous and flowing, and madness came riding in on the moon; there I could have this girl any way she wanted, pulling out all the stops, doing what had to be done. Yes, then I could really bust out—then I'd make her head spin. *You want summa Wes? You got it baby, you got it all you want. You just say the word...*

My hand reached out, grabbing hold of her fluffy little ass, firmly cupping the left cheek; I pulled her close and this evil kind of smile came over my face. "I'll be back later," I told her. "But right now I've gotta go, I gotta *be* somewhere..."

She seemed truly sad. Or annoyed, I don't know which.

"Well, are you coming back?" she asked. "Please, soon?"

I only laughed, fetching my cigarettes and sparking one up. "So what's the big hurry? Lookit, I don't even know your name..."

She slung out her arms, gluing her body to my own and pushing two pouty lips to one ear. "*My name is Marcelle*," she whispered, and ran her tongue along the side of my neck...

"There," she said simply, pulling away, as if she'd tossed a newspaper over a puddle of dog piss. "Now you know my name. You know my name and now we're not strangers...that is, *if* you'll tell me yours. Will you, Weston? Tell me your name...?"

But I just cocked a grin, doing that bank robber bit again with the eyes. "You'll just have to wait and see, now won't you, baby?"

Boy, can you say some stupid things to women sometimes. Half the time I don't think we even realize what we're saying, I really don't. We just get that dizzy feeling around the ears and then our mouths are moving only there's no sound, just those terrible blue eyes and those long endless legs and, oh, have mercy...

"When?" she asked, one hand caressing down my face and past the tiny cluster of scars smattering my left eye. Her fingers felt warm and soft.

I brushed my lips to hers. "Tonight," I told her, the word like a starting gun as Marcelle swooped in, jamming her sweet little tongue practically down my throat. I stumbled back, almost tripping out the door until my fingers caught the itch and went grabbing for warm skin and bulges. Just as my hand was creeping up the front of her shirt, she pulled away.

"*Tonight?*" she asked, her breath coming sharper now, gasping almost. "*Do you promise?*"

"I promise."

"Do you really, Wes, or are you just saying

that?"

"I'd be a fool if I was," I told her, then gave a lopsided grin as she stepped back, lighting a smoke she'd lifted from my pack. When she was finished, Marcelle returned the grin with a wry smile of her own and then tossed back the lighter, chucking it right at my chest, and I gave her this wild-eyes look that said *You're fuckin' crazy, you know that? But that's all right, 'cause sometimes I like crazy. I'm crazy too*, and then stepped outside, a soft breeze rushing my face and highlighting the spit smeared there like cool, knowing fingerprints. I wiped a hand at my mouth and took a deep breath.

Like I said: *make her head spin.*

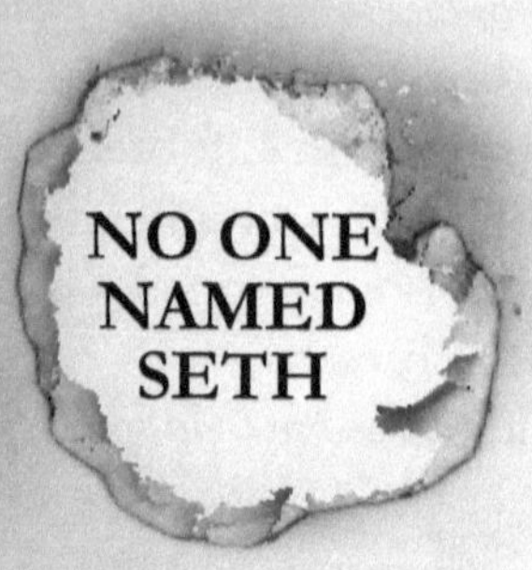

The afternoon went fast.
Searching the baggie from the night before, I saw that, in addition to the weed, Prentice had slipped me some assorted skittles, as well—muscle relaxers, I think—and I promptly swallowed a few of these down, setting in motion a wave I hoped to ride well into the night.

These types of handouts were not uncommon from Prentice. The town's more notorious denizens had for years made a habit of stuffing substances into practically every orifice of his body, and when my cousin gave he was only giving from his abundance. The laymen made the usual schwag offerings, of course, but the dealers...well, they had slipped Prentice the keys to the kingdom.

Besides, he was great publicity.

Most of the day I spent on the couch, sipping miso and jamming tunes and watching the tube. Then I'd grab Prentice's baggie and swallow another pill, just chillin'-like. Then I went and found this book I'd been reading called *I Was Taken*, one of those true-story deals about this farmer who, pitch-fork in hand, had confronted some UFOs she claims knocked off a couple of her prize-winning cattle. Funny story.

Only then I'd turned a page and opened my eyes and realized I was stumbling down Kershaw Road, my head feeling obscenely dented and swollen against the hot evening air. I'd gone as far as Oyster Boulevard when I noticed duallys and flat-beds jolting out of parking lots and down narrow side streets, then followed along as many threw the turn into Ernul's and dragged their feet inside, the streets filled for a moment with sad stretched-out laughter and Barbie doll squeals.

It was Friday night and, dependable as always, the crowds were out in full force. Not many new faces—the birthday boy sipping Pabst at the bar, and next to him some geezer with rheumy eyes and a Fu Manchu—but plenty of familiars, including most of the ornery loggers from the night before and Reelsboro County's small but dedicated club of divorced middle-agers. And there was Diane Struthers's mom, who used to be married to Kevin Hillebrandt, now with her new hamburger-head boyfriend, and Bradley Dubbins, probably the greatest quarterback in Bayboro High history. And over in the corner was Antoine Remarks, Johnny Remarks's brother, who wasn't as big around in the waist as Johnny but just as thickheaded when it came to knowing when to clam up.

I caught a glimpse of Spike, puffing a cigarette from our corner in the back and singing snatches of "Midnight Rider." The payphone on the wall had been ringing since I walked in, and now someone answered and was screaming *"Seth! Seth! Se-eth!"* Then he said, "Pal, they ain't no *Seth* here," and hung up. Buster saw me and approached the open side of the bar, where I slapped a few bucks in his pocket and he handed over an icy cold six-pack.

Slowly I edged through the crowd, moving past the bar when, as if on cue, I heard the first of the stools creak and then swivel behind my back, bodies turning in their seats. Throats were cleared.

I knew what was coming.

"Hay Wes. Where's that crazy cousin a yurs?"

"That boy gonna be making any a that racket up 'er tonight?"

"Yeah Wes, is Prentice playing tonight? Is he?"

I stumbled slightly, the weight of the beers making me lopsided as I turned to the bar. Everyone was quiet.

"Well," I said, "I just don't think that's going to be possible, I'm afraid. You see, the gennies are bone dry, and what and all with the double-shows Prentice has been pulling, I just don't think he's going to quite have the money to fill them this weekend. But, with enough saving—and a little luck—he may be able to have 'em gassed up and ready to go maybe by next weekend—"

"Next *weekend?*"

"—or possibly the end of the month, that is if—"

And everybody said *the end of the month!* and then were squirming in their seats, feeling at pockets and reaching for their last swig of beer. Hank Sawyer whipped out his wallet and dangled a ten-spot at my free hand.

"Here," he said.

"Give him this," said another, this one a twenty. More sprouts of cash blossomed down the line: ones, fives, another ten.

I grabbed the floating bills and stuffed them in my jeans.

"You tell him Hank Sawyer is having open-heart surgery Monday morning, and I'd be much obliged if he would fill those tanks before then."

"Yes sir," I said. "I surely will."

Suddenly a look came over old Hank's face, a lovely, wearied look. "And you tell him I love it when he sings. That I ain't never heard nothing like it, not in all my life."

Snickers.

"I mean that," he growled. "I really do. Nobody but my wife can sing something so beautiful as what that boy can."

A lady's head bobbed in over my shoulder.

"And you tell him he needs to call Janelle. Tell him the laundromat just ain't the same without him."

"I'll definitely see what I can do." I raised my sixer in a small wave. "Keep your ears open, fellas. Ma'am."

I'd got maybe three steps from the bar when this girl Bridget snuck up from behind, her soft body politely blocking my way.

"Wes, did Prentice *really* run out of gas?"

I forced her back to the table, propping the sixer on the edge of our booth.

"He really did. Scouts honor," I said, showing my palm.

Her eyes narrowed. "I think you're full of shit."

Always a sharp one, that Bridget. Ugly as homemade soap, but sharp. We'd come real close to kissing one night out in the alley that summer.

"*Well*," I said, moving in on her face, "*I think the show's starting early tonight, so you'd better get up there and fast if you want a good seat.*"

Bridget beamed a secret smile and scurried off, whispering excitedly as she joined her friends near the door.

"Looks like we're gonna need a bigger boat," I said, sliding into the booth. My eyes skimmed the row of bodies lining the counter, smoke swirling in one misty wave along ceiling. "Look at this place, doesn't anybody drink at *home* anymore?"

Spike snorted, swiping a blistered hand across his forehead. "Been a long week, Wes...guess everybody needs a break."

"You're still going tonight, right?"

Spike nodded. "Still going, soon as I finish a couple these-here beers."

"Well, I think it'd be best for us both if we get a move on, A-sap."

"What's the hurry?"

I cracked open my bottle and scoped the bar, watching as smoke danced from the rafters and the merrymakers rejoiced, waiting like the rest us for the music, for the night, for the ride to begin.

"No hurry," I told him. "Just make it snappy, will ya?"

§

For as long as I'd known him, Spike had never owned a car. Once upon a time he had—nothing special, a Pinto I believe—though after three DWIs and another incident involving a stolen go-cart, the state had been quick to bang the gavel, sending Spike out the other side as a permanent pedestrian. And though he'd earned these stripes honestly enough, I'd always suspected they were part of the reason we'd hit it off so well, each of us generously acquainted with the looks of warm apathetic faces as they drove past in the rain, safe in their cocoon of molded steel and glass.

We stopped to grab a couple bags of ice on our way to the Creek Road, carrying them along as we crossed the Yard and could already hear traces of the band tuning up and riff-doodling, tossing down echoes over the town. Mufflers roared past as crowds of beer-handed parents herded along their children, one floppy-breasted mother screaming wild to a young boy lapping in the canal. We kept moving and were halfway to the top when the amps choked out a scream and finally Olympus landed, raining down a symphony of blood-and-guts pentatonics and pounding hellhound drums that made me think of Marcelle.

The candles burned brightly as we walked inside, guiding us along while we went pouring ice into coolers. The Two Mad Gennies rumbled from their roost near the stage, pumping blood to the guitars and up the mike stand, out through the amps and finally down the mountain itself, the room turned electric and brimming with an unholy mixture of testosterone and smoke and abandon.

Like a gargoyle awakened from his stare of stone, Prentice stalked the stage in androgynous glory, hair swimming in long, shining curls down his back. Dark shadows bulged beneath his eyes and cheek bones; sweat lifted from his pores. His dark Ibanez Destroyer slung low at his waist, Prentice sang and screamed the drunken woes of the world, no longer an artist but a pained scribe of human sorrow.

The dark opera had begun.

Spike nudged me, baring a toothy grin as he waved a finger and then vanished through the crowd. Only then something happened—the pills, maybe, or the miso, or any of the other myriad things that make a person crazy—but watching him go suddenly my vision was shattered, the room disintegrating to fragments and then slowly, magically coming together again: a curious jigsaw puzzle of perception.

I watched helplessly as the scene repeated it-self—a second time, and a third—feeling somehow naked and the pressure building fast in my knees and then finally letting loose. I staggered awkward-ly, a sudden guttural croak rising from within as I tilted clumsily over, crashing to the floor. Faces turned back to me, exchanging whispers, mutters, stares.

Everything went dark.

The final chord of "Silver String" withered away, consumed by a fresh row of cheers from the crowd; without delay the bass cranked into the next number, notes creeping sinuously from the speak-ers as Prentice's voice swam down the mountain:

Who is your master
and who can ya trust
when your enemies are fightin'
and there's nowhere left to run

In the ground, cold and still
bodies...turnin' white
this dream of mine, it seems so real
while something screams inside:

cast that die,
cast that die

Cowards gathered t'gether
and the best of men've died
world full a hatred
the worst a men survive

cast that die,
cast that die

Still I raise my drink t'night
to dream instead a think
of that dreary day tomorrow
I say I'd rather sleep

A burgeoning chaos swept the room, subtly pervading the air with its raw blend of lunacy and hysteria; at any moment, it seemed, the roof would shatter and be taken by the fury, the power, the *will* of the music. All around me there was talking and screaming and laughter, and raising my eyes a sudden beam of light flashed golden from a nearby shelf and—

And that's when I saw it.

Saw something that *should've* been Marcelle, maybe doing naked calisthenics or swinging from a pole, going *down down down*—should've been, but it wasn't. It wasn't her at all. What I saw instead— *was Spike.* Sad, pseudo-paternal Spike, crushing out a cigarette and then bumbling through the crowd; Spike, with his sniper-scope glasses and filthy work hat, moving out the door and softly into the night and down the pass, walking away, leaving me...

As quickly as it had come the vision faded, vanishing against the candlelit haze of the barn, and again I caught that sudden flash of gold from the corner of one eye. As the music played, I struggled to my feet, stumbling to the old shelf and the pair of battered brass knuckles waiting for me there. I took them in my hands, trying them on, and—though the fit was a little loose—slipped them into my pocket.

Not far from the shelf I spotted a cooler, and hopping on top got a quick bird's-eye view of Bob slamming at his bass, and Prentice writhing like a snake on center stage. I spotted Bridget and her bunch dancing near the door...lanky James Harrell and the AP crew...Lil' Dee staring out a window... and there, slouched sexily before the stage—Marcelle, her blonde hair shining in the darkness, swimming down her face and over her fierce, sculpted breasts.

I took her in once more, took in the way she tipped that tallboy to the ceiling and swallowed it whole, the dazed beauty of those beautiful clown eyes. Through the long hours of the day I'd somehow convinced myself she wasn't real at all, that she'd only been imagined, a living dream; but now I watched her, loved her, *ached* down in my soul for her, drinking her in as a depraved man would a cup of cold water in the desert.

Go for it Wes, give her what you got. Spank that girl like her daddy never could...

And then, amidst this burning and aching and throbbing, through this spiraling haze of dreadful lust and desire, I saw...

Spike.

Not on the couch, or lost in the crowd, but again on that splintered screen of the mind, sweeping down the trail and now out into the Yard. And just like that, seeing him go, I knew in a very simple way that I had no choice but to follow.

Prentice screamed something into the microphone, loud, unintelligible words that sent shivers through the audience. A great peal of laughter shook the room, echoed by shouts and upraised arms.

I stepped off the cooler.

One leg started for Marcelle and the thunder of the Two Mad Gennies.

The other held heavy, unmoving.

Not happening, it said.

Well, fuck me, I thought.

After a final lingering glance to the stage, I turned and headed for the door...

DOWN
THE
MOUNTAIN

Couples lay sprawled on blankets beside ravaged cases of beer, some with kiddies running wild or asleep on a bed of grass; others lounged in cracked contour chairs or hung out of truck cabs. I stumbled past them on my way across the Yard, past drooping tents strung up along the gorge—and still no Spike. Through the sloppy middle with its mess of mud and motors and slow-dancing elders—no Spike. I'd looked everywhere, remembering the splintered vision from earlier, and found—nothing.

I'd started back for the trees when I spotted him, milling around the remains of an absurdly-colored pickup and surrounded by a nuclear family of Mexicans and another, much smaller man in neat-looking clothes. The Mexican I recognized as Taco, one of Vanceboro's small-time grass dealers; the other man I had met but couldn't remember his name. I strolled over, coming close enough to whiff the beer on their breath when all at once Spike slapped wildly at his knee, the entire group crumbling into hysterics.

I had apparently arrived just in time to miss the joke.

Then they'd settled down and I was introduced, first to Taco and then the younger-looking man in nice clothes, whose name was Honoré Lafargue but who everybody called Ray, just plain Ray, as in *do-re-mi*. I nodded politely to both and Taco, teetering now on the tailgate of his Nissan, whistled over an attractive Mexican woman with thin eyebrows.

"Honey, get Wes here a beer. Can't you see his throat is parched?"

She blasted something in Spanish, I couldn't tell what it was. Something sarcastic though, not mean, but playful.

"*Woman, whom do you think you are? Taking that malicious-like tone with me?*" Taco cocked a crazy eyebrow. "*Don't make me take off my belt, give you a spankin'...*"

They smiled tender, drunken smiles at each other, the woman staggering over and reaching through the cab's open window, revealing a beer. She handed it to her husband.

"You're going to be the one getting the *spanking*," she threatened.

"If I'm lucky," he said, slurring. "I bet you will give me a little pank-pank, *won't choo?*"

Taco's eyes lolled drowsily to my own and he cocked a smile, as if he'd said that one just for me, old buddy old pal. Then he tossed me the beer and said *drink up* and, before I got a word in edge-wise, the well-oiled motor of their conversation was already cranked and rumbling down the road.

For the next forty-five minutes I listened as they swapped stories, slyly bragging about all the stupid things they'd managed to cram into one sucky life, and some they'd apparently been through together. Soon it was too much and I thought if I had to summon even one more phony laugh—just one—my head would explode. I'd tried everything, every kind of ignorant laugh you could think of: I'd done a down-deep Santa Claus laugh—like *ho! ho! ho!*—and this lighter laugh, a half-chuckle really, sort of like a scoff. I'd done my heavy-on-the-tongue laugh, sort of *tss-tss-tss*, like a snake, and I'd pulled out the old reverse psychology laugh, where it sounds so obviously fake it *has* to be real. I'd even done this really embarrassing *explosion!* of a laugh where it was like I even sort of surprised *myself* with it. It was all planned though.

I'd done it all, folks, and the ironic thing was *nothing was really even that funny.* Really though, who cares how many Spanish bar fights you've been in, or how much shattered glass you have floating in your bloodstream? Or how many times you could give us the eye around your wife's back without overtly saying you'd had an affair? And, frankly, if you got drunk on Tequila 1800 and did that to *my* front yard with a tractor, I'd probably shoot you with a .22 as well. For her part Taco's wife never said much, but she couldn't *stop* laughing, and as if that wasn't bad enough, then she started *crying*. Good golly.

Occasionally I'd glance over at Spike, and when he wasn't laughing—more and more as time wore on—occasionally his eyes seemed to fade into the back of his head, and I don't think he would've known much more if his thin little jacket had burst into flames with him inside it. Mostly, though, I watched the children, two little girls with sweet dark eyes, staring in drunken wonder as they spun crashing circles in the open field. I felt an ominous empathy for those girls, a foreboding sadness over the world they'd been born into and in which they'd one day have to survive, the last gleam of innocence finally sinking out of those same—but much different—dark eyes.

Ray, meanwhile, was going on about the music, claiming to have never in all his life heard anything as beautiful nor captivating. He went on and on about it—especially about Prentice and his voice, which he described as "one of those voices you dream of after birth, and hear a little before death," going on to say that throughout life this voice becomes more and more an "idea to the ears." As he spoke, his eyes occasionally cast a weird constipated look, as if he were about to cry. And just when

I thought he would, just when I was sure he was breaking down and about to burst—his face would change, fading again to that innocent virgin smile.

He was still going on about it when a beer-gutted man in checked flannel and flip-flops stuttered over and started yelling "Howdy!" and "How *do?*" and glad-handing everybody. Whatever I'd come here for—whatever that splintery, jigsaw vision had meant—surely it wasn't this, and presently I spoke a hurried g'bye and took off across the field.

I hadn't gone far before running into Billy Gilmour, who lived over in Cranston, and in exchange for some pills swapped him the brass knucks I'd pocketed earlier. I crunched two of the tablets there, tucking away the rest for later; Billy blew a hot belch and staggered on down the strip. Finally, turning again to the music, a vivid snapshot of Marcelle's crotch rose teasingly in my head and lingered, sending a violent jolt to my groin as I started up the pass...

§

I ran as fast and for as long as I could.

Through the towering pines and up the pass, the moon casting its pale glow through the trees as I neared the final rise and felt a sharp pain riding up my guts. My stomach clunked, dropping me to my knees as the music swelled, tapered, died out. Then I jumped to my feet and took off, dreaming softly about Marcelle and sad clowns and the feeling of being watched through the trees until finally Bob and Prentice appeared up ahead, each coddled by groupies as they started down the mountain.

It was the middle of the set.

The time when Prentice descended to mingle with his loyal subjects, and receive their burnt offerings of low smiles and complimentary dope.

We traded a few slurred grunts as they passed, and frantically I scanned the group for a pair of brilliant blues, but there were none. Then they were gone, the crowd marching onward in a cloud of swinging shadows and firefly cherries, and looking after them the pines appeared curved and slippery, leaning at awkward angles from the earth.

"What about Marcelle!" I called after them.

Laughing, an indiscriminate holler.

"Think she's still inside!" came a hope.

"Yuh! She's in the house!"

That was all I needed, leaping like a madman as I tore up the pass. *Please don't leave*, I heard her say, and the voice was low and cracking, as if spoken from years ago. *I've been up for an hour now...I'm bored...*

Oh just you wait baby, I'll be your huckleberry...

I crashed inside, the room somehow darker now despite the candles, and straining my eyes I noticed faces passed out on a nearby couch, a few more on the floor, none of them Marcelle. I crept to the stage, discovering her empty tallboy abandoned by a lumpy rag-tattered quilt. As I watched, the quilt rose and fell in my vision, something breathing underneath.

"Hey you..." I whispered, already picturing her

warm body nestled beneath, calling, calling for my touch; I peered down, and in the shifting shadows saw...

Nothing. An empty beer can, some quarters and change.

I lifted the can, turning it in my hands when the silence was broken by a sudden knocking—faint at first, growing louder as I stumbled within feet of the small closet behind the stage.

Prentice's room.

The door was closed.

Then a sudden, moaning squeal from inside—followed by laughter, high and garrulous, the familiar tones of it carrying through the slab of wood and stopping me cold as the whole damn charade came crashing down, two parts of my brain latching together like two pieces of a puzzle that were never meant to fit.

No...NONONONO

But it was.

It was and I knew it, and without thinking put my ear to the door; listening closer, I could now make out another voice—a deep, brooding sort of grunt. And though this additional role player was in no way a surprise, the fact of his existence filled me with a rage that, in that moment, was hard to comprehend.

Ohhhhh

Ohh yesssssss

I spun, stomping like a three-year-old from behind the stage and past the waving hands of candles burning in the darkness. I'd almost reached the front door when I tripped on something, saw it was a cooler, then reared back and swung a kick that toppled it recklessly and sent a stream of ice and water spilling over the floor. A flotilla of beer cans rode the wave, and one by one I snatched these up and in the next moment was surprised to find myself tossing them, slinging the cans as adeptly as a drunken Nolan Ryan through the shattered barn windows.

Slam!

Crash!

Bodies were starting to wake and move around, coughing, groaning, mumbling. I turned, screaming for them to shut up ya bastards, shut your dirty fuckin' mouths, then stormed outside and over to the old banana-seat bike that'd been rotting into the barn since sometime around the end of Roosevelt. I grabbed hold of its handlebars, yanking the withered tires free of the weeds and then hoisting the whole rusty mess over my head and flinging it into a tree, a jagged piece of its sissy bar catching on my hand as it went airborne through the night.

I looked, and through the sudden fog saw a glob of darkness swelling in my palm.

Then came the pain.

I screamed, long and loud, the noise of it pouring out of me as easily as the blood poured from my hand, wrapping it in a dark, warming mitten. Slowly I came to the realization that, yes, I was light-headed, and check, growing weaker by the second, and for one fleeting moment knew the pain was not pain at all, but actually this terrible new drug that made my mind dart back and forth, sputtering with despair.

You're gonna pass out ya know, you keep standing around like this...

I need a beer, a shot, some green sticky weed...

You're gonna pass out Wes, and those idiots are gonna try and shave your head and defecate on your chest. They'll do it. They're that sick.

A cigarette, a benny, anything, gimme what ya got...

On your chest.

I ripped out of my shirt, wrapping it carefully around my hand. The moon sailed from behind a cloud, and with it my body regressed into some primal state, muscles tensing, legs pumping like machinery as they carried me down the pass...

I hadn't got far when I heard voices, laughter, people moving up ahead. Without thinking I made a hard left into the woods, slipping in the straw, getting up, running. And somewhere through it all, through this haze of blood and rage and double vision, I heard the endless groans of the Norfolk Southern freight pushing slowly through town.

I would spend the next hour stumbling blindly through the darkness of the forest, blood drying to a sick brown crust that glued my shirt to my palm. I took the steep side down the mountain, emptying onto a black sky over Highway 55, and upon reaching the street could already hear the music growling once more, slowly fading as I hobbled home, just another bleeding soul, another stumbling shadow in the night...

Sunlight fell in arcs over the railroad, perfect shining blades that transformed the bottles and shattered glass to an ethereal snowfall as I moved down the Norfolk Southern line. Birds called down from the pines, the only noises this far back, and despite the rising smell of the garbage bags slung over one shoulder, I couldn't help but feel I'd discovered a little slice of paradise back in these woods.

I'd been walking for miles, the journey a familiar one that, despite its natural wonders, usually worked holy hell on my knees. So far they hadn't complained, however, and not pushing my luck I let down the bags and popped a squat in the grass, glancing to the long Cali-shaped scar down my palm. The gash had gotten much uglier over the last three weeks and only now, in the golden sun, did it finally appear to be healing.

Three weeks, I thought. *Seems like three years...*

I'd spent this time alone, and in its wake the memory of that night had slipped slowly away, growing eternally fuzzy and faded. Evening had come soon that next day, and though I didn't listen for the music I knew Prentice was back at it again, sweating, pulsing, pounding his way to sunrise. Going out in one more everlasting blaze of glory before his body finally shut down and left him unconscious, stowed away like some stiffening corpse in that room to the back, that vacuous little closet where—

(ohhhhh ohhh yesssssss)

Stop it.

Just stop.

If anything, the past three weeks had kept me well-versed in the knowledge that only time could heal so many of life's little scars, that occasionally the madman within arises and draws us swiftly from the humanity on which we'd once depended. My life had gone suddenly black-and-white, a glorious but sordid splendor, and I was in no mood for anyone sniffing around and wondering where all the color had gone. Didn't want them breathing down my neck or trying to buy me another beer. The scar may've been physical but something else—something bigger, deeper—had changed *inside*, something that skirted words proper but whose presence could not be ignored: a dark bearing-down of emotion that spun the world to something flat, a drab parade on a rainy day, and whenever it marched into town my head could not convince my heart that I was not, in fact, a turtle.

Some nights I followed these same tracks, winding through the pines and past Goose Creek, into Arapahoe, sometimes as far as Riverside. Hunched between the trees, I smoked homegrown and wept without care and watched the Norfolk Southern go howling carelessly through the night, yelling in that terrible voice that sounded so much like a dying harmonica. And what would happen, I wondered, if you passed out on those tracks? Would the ringing whistles wake you up? Or would you only hear the distant clinks of the freight bell tolling for thee and then suddenly get that feeling of someone rolling you up in an unbearably thick blanket and then—*nothing.*

When it was finished I tossed down the Marlboro, then hoisted the bags and started back down the tracks. The late August air was hot and holding to summer, the chill of that week having been blown with the clouds farther south, and by the time I reached the faded dumpster out back the Shop Quick my shoes felt squishy and swollen with sweat. Commandeering local dumpsters for personal use wasn't my favorite thing in the world to do, believe me, but it was still better than burning the stuff in a pile in my backyard—something I'd almost got a citation for the previous spring.

Afterwards I crept around and went inside, the battered silver bell shaking its tuneless rattle as I walked through the door. I spotted some of the local dealers leaning near the coolers and went over, glad-handing everybody, *what's good, what's good?* Scuba Steve, the coolest of the bunch, saw me and slipped a baggie in my shirt pocket. Then I passed through the dinky little checkout and out the door, trying best as I could to carry all those bags—two cartons of Marlboros, some microwave dinners, case of Budweiser—with one hand. I was still fumbling with it all when I heard a distant horn—*BONK-BONK BONK-BOOOOONK*—and turning saw an old Datsun sputtering away down the road, muffler razzing and popping in a series of backfires as the ghost of an arm reached out its window...and, yes, it must've been my name I heard called out through the smoke; then only the faint shrill of somebody yelling, yelling about...about what?

And at who—yelling at *me? YELLING AT ME?*

I charged stupidly forward, spilling cigarettes and cheap spaghetti dinners and flipping them the bird. For a long moment it held high and flying as I screeched after them, something taunting and mildly Oedipal.

Then they were gone.

Gathering my things, I glanced once more down the road and then started for the trees, and the long walk home that lay ahead.

§

An hour later I'd walked inside and dropped the bags on the counter, and was still putting things away when I heard a motor and looked to see, of all things, a DeLorean parked out front; then came the knocking, and with it a wisp of curly dark hair moving back and forth through faded panes in the front door. I tried remembering anyone I knew or had ever met who owned a DeLorean, but then suddenly the knocks gave way to silence and the screen door closed and I did my best to peep through the blinds.

She was off the porch and halfway to her car when I snatched open the door and the woman turned, a bewildered sort of look on her face.

"Weston? Is that you?"

I crossed tentatively to the edge of the steps. "Hey, Aunt Joyce..."

"Weston! I was just *sure* I'd driven all this way and come to the *wrong* house!" Moving in her standard penguin waddle, Aunt Joyce rushed the porch and there was a deep, awful silence as we strategically embraced. The thick smell of perfume ran up my nostrils, leaving a stench I would be catching in whiffs and hints for the rest of the night. "How've you been, sweetheart?"

I lied a little about how I'd been and we smiled at each other for a good couple of minutes and said a lot of the predictable things family members say when they're nervous and haven't seen each other in well over two hundred years: she went on about how much I'd *grown*, and how *skinny* I was, and how *long* my hair had gotten. Then she'd rub my little chin and tell me I needed to shave that peach fuzz before a cat came along and licked it off.

She looked like she'd come straight from a funeral home, makeup caked-on like a china doll and wearing a dark formal dress that just sort of rolled with the punches. We stood there a moment in silence until I noticed the first burp of sweat on her forehead and realized this was not an occasional in-the-area stopover, that I had no choice but to ask her inside.

I turned on some lights and poured a glass of tea while she waited on the couch, only afterwards remembering the stockpile of beer and cigarettes on the kitchen counter. A little embarrassed, I fished out the dinners and stuck them in the freezer and then walked over, handed Aunt Joyce her tea.

"Thank you, kind sir," she said, her eyes doing a number over the various prints I'd tacked up along the living room walls.

"I like Dalí," I explained, taking a seat.

"Mm, I can tell." She pointed to a framed picture behind my back. "The Escher blends in well, it's a nice touch." I nodded, and after settling her glass Aunt Joyce turned her eyes briefly toward the kitchen and said, "Weston, son, please don't tell me you've moved all this way just to become another one of these local knuckleheads."

I curved my lip and stared at the floor.

"*Mercy!*" she gasped, dropping her head in a great sarcasm of anguish. "You boys are bad as sailors with your Budweiser and your stinky old *cigars*—you and Prentice both! Jesus help them all!"

Oh no, here it comes...

See, something about Aunt Joyce, she was born-again. Sort of a Bible-thumper. Not that it was any secret or anything, anybody who ever talked to the woman for five minutes could tell you that. It was magical in a way, 'cause no matter what was being said Aunt Joyce had this uncanny ability to link everything to "the Lord"—I mean, you could be talking about the way bugs kiss your windshield and next breath she'd pick up with bloodshed and salvation. You'd be making an intentionally neutral comment on the sucky weather, and she'd go off on times and seasons and endless tribulation. I thought it was probably the most annoying thing about her, and started to ask what she thought about her buddy Jim Bakker now, what she had to say about all her little Sunday buddies over at the PTL scandal, but I stopped myself. What's the point.

"God's got bigger plans for you than this," she said, brushing her hand at the kitchen counter. "You're too *smart* for this stuff, Weston."

"Yeah, I know, Aunt Joyce."

"No, you don't. Do you remember the night I visited you in that hospital?"

"I remember."

"Do you remember when I prayed over you?

Do you remember what I said?"

"Yes, ma'am. Most of it."

"Good. Now it may not mean much to you, but when God speaks nature and eternity listen, and there ain't nothing you can do to change it. You were meant for a higher purpose, don't ever forget that. God loves you, Weston, you are the very center of His universe—now stop being so wayward and come on home!"

I just nodded, awkward as hell. "Yes, ma'am."

"How're your legs? They still give you trouble?"

"Ah...not really. I mean, when it rains it pours. And sometimes if I walk too far my knees get kind of...powdery."

"Well! Maybe if you got yourself a car you wouldn't have to *walk* so much, you think?" Aunt Joyce shook her head and laughed, a thick, all-consuming howl. "I couldn't believe my ears, your momma told me you were still walking everywhere."

"It's really easier to walk..."

"It's *cheaper* to walk, is what you mean to say."

"It also happens to be cheaper," I consented, "this is true."

"*Mm-hmm.*"

"You're not going to change my mind on this, Aunt Joyce. I'm an unabashed pedestrian and I refuse to give in to the conspiratorial fascism of insurance companies. I just won't do it."

Aunt Joyce squinted her eyes, doing her best to hold back a smile. "I'd rather you drive a car than a wheelchair, sweetheart."

"Well, I could always take that sassy ride off your hands." I made a face. "A *DeLorean?*"

"Freddie's idea. I hate it. Don't get one."

Just then I thought of something. "Aunt Joyce, do you know anybody who drives a white Datsun?"

"A Datsun?" she asked. "No honey, I don't know anybody with a Datsun, not anybody who ain't been dead and gone for the past ten years. Why? See one you like?"

"No, I was just—"

"What happened to your hand?"

I glanced to my palm, not really wanting to. Hoping it didn't look as bad as it felt. "Nothing... cut it on some metal."

"Boy! You better get a Tetanus shot for that."

"How's Mom?"

"Worried. About you."

"Why worry?" I asked, not stopping a smile. "I'm not dying."

Aunt Joyce sighed.

"She's your mother, Weston, and you're her little boy," she told me. "Don't act so surprised. Besides, it ain't right for you to do your mother this way, you know that. You should at least call her sometime—she spent eighteen years raising you, she ain't gonna forget about you just like that. As good as that may sound to you."

"Yeah, I know." I was sort of mumbling. "Has my dad finished the cruiser yet?"

"No! Are you crazy?"

"And Uncle Fred?" I asked. "How're things at Weyerhaeuser?"

"Freddie got saved, Weston."

I actually laughed when I heard it—it was an automatic response. Aunt Joyce only smiled gently, however, quiet, and instantly my mind moved back to so many memories of Uncle Fred, memories long since fogged by time. Hard as I tried, I couldn't imagine Uncle Fred throwing so much as a passing glance at a church, much less stepping foot inside. When Aunt Joyce got weird, he swore up and down he'd *never* get religion, had even hinted at divorce. It was Uncle Fred who'd let Prentice drop out of school at sixteen and, two months later, when Prentice decided he'd just as soon move out as spend another day at home, it was Uncle Fred who let him.

"It took Freddie *fourteen years* to finally surrender his life to the Lord," she said, picking at her dress. A thick glass had formed over her eyes. "But that just goes to show if Freddie can ask God into his heart, anybody can. *Anybody*," she choked. "Even my son..."

For a moment everything was quiet, until finally Aunt Joyce pulled a Kleenex from her purse, wiping at her eyes. She said, "Weston, what's the matter with him?"

"With who? You mean Prentice?"

She nodded, and I thought for a moment, puffing away the cigarette I'd lit and struggling for something useful to say. Only, looking at her now, a great pity welled up like balloons in my chest and suddenly all I saw was this sad little woman too wrapped up in loving her son for her own good.

"I don't know," I answered lamely. And I didn't. Prentice was definitely different, no doubt in that; he just had this problem with pushing limits, that's all. And although I'd never told him this, a part of me honestly didn't expect him to make it to thirty. "I mean, you know how Prentice is, Aunt Joyce. He just likes doing his own thing."

"I know, I know," she said, still dabbing at her eyes. "He always has, ever since he was a child he's wanted things his own way." She smiled emptily, her eyes dancing into the distance. "Sometimes I would catch him just...staring off at the sun..."

I grinned, remembering the time I was fourteen and Prentice had taught me, too, how to stare down the sun. *The trick*, he'd said, *is not to blink*. Then he'd demonstrated for me, gazing almost two minutes straight into the glory, never blinked once...

"I know he's peculiar," Aunt Joyce said, "but what's *happening* to him, Weston, why is he *acting* this way? I just know he's the one who attacked that boy..."

My hand stopped cold over the ash tray. Distantly I heard the pattering of rain at the window, at times fast and hard, then pulling back to whispers. "What boy?"

"The Harrell boy?" She looked at me, surprised. "Didn't you know?"

"Well...I haven't really talked to Prentice in a few days, Aunt Joyce. What happened?"

"Oh, I don't know," she said, exhausted. "Some boy got beat up the other night up near that cabin where he stays—up on that *mountain* of his."

She'd got my attention, at least. "And this was when?"

"It happened on the twentieth, so that would've been...Thursday? A boy named James Harrell. Do you know him?"

Yes. James Harrell. Brainiac from Bayboro High.

"The name sounds familiar..."

"Well, he's in the hospital. Three cracked ribs, apparently, and a broken nose, possible concussion." Aunt Joyce composed herself, as if preparing to give an official statement: "All's they said was he was attacked in those woods, where I don't know. Said the boy was filthy drunk and claims it was too dark to see who it was, but I just *know*...I just *know* that..." Now her face began to flap and quiver as the tears started back, slipping down her cheeks.

But I wouldn't believe it, couldn't. No way would Prentice do that—and if he had, there must've been a *reason*; Prentice was a lot of things, but violent was not one of them. A thief, yeah; a drunk, an addict, you bet; a pusher, sometimes. But true violence had never been a part of Prentice's vocabulary, and the more I thought about it the more I realized what a dangerous ingredient it would be to someone like Prentice's life. Prentice had an entire county of people who would fight and probably die for him...but what if that wasn't enough? What if he wanted to eat just for the sake of tasting? Like he'd ate orgies and freedom, like he'd ate pride and drugs and rebellion? And now, what if he ate murder? What if he ate *death?*

Leaning forward with renewed determination, Aunt Joyce pointed a finger to nowhere and said, "I may not be able to drive my car up that mountain, Weston...but my prayers go *straight to heaven!*"

I crushed my cigarette, got up and moved beside her on the couch. I wanted to comfort and soothe her and tell her everything was gonna be all right; I wanted her to stay calm, stop *crying.* But I simply couldn't think of anything to say to this woman I previously knew so well but who now seemed so much like a stranger. And as lightning flashed through the blinds and thunder rolled heavy over the hills and came rattling at the walls, Aunt Joyce got that funny look in her eyes and began whispering: *"The devil's tryna kill my little boy...he's a murderer, Weston, but he won't take 'im...you hear that, he won't take 'im, my God won't let him..."*

I squirmed nervously, my arm feeling suddenly out of place where it sat on Aunt Joyce's shoulder. Her eyes stared into space, forever lost and wild, until finally she snatched her purse and fumbled inside, I thought for another Kleenex, finally revealing a book instead.

"Give this to him. Tell him I love him."

I took the book in my hands, saw the title

scrawled across the cover: *Paths to God*. A few bookmarks poked from inside and some of the pages had been dog-eared, but other than that it looked almost new.

"There's a letter in there for him," she said, and I noticed an envelope near the end of the book. She reached into her purse again, this time drawing a small plastic bottle. "Thank God for Advil," she said, and swallowed two tablets with a gulp of tea.

For several moments she cleaned at her face with the tissue, dabbing her eyes, then told me she had to leave and pick up Uncle Fred from Word Study or Men's Night or some other Holier Than Thou seminar, said she knew I was tired of her moping. I didn't want to tell her she was right. She asked me to please call my mom, told me she still prayed for me every day, and that I was too smart to be throwing my life away. And then she left.

I waved goodbye from the porch, watching as the DeLorean crept ominously down the road and out of sight. Walking inside, for a long moment I stood staring over the living room with its spiderwebs and stains, at Aunt Joyce's miserable glass of tea and the beer growing warm on the kitchen counter. And seeing it all, that deep sadness became a little more real and I thought it would've been nice if Aunt Joyce had maybe stuck around after all, just a little while longer, and I started to cry.

LOCAL STRANGERS

Spike showed up later that week, appearing on my porch just as the sun sank low behind Prentice's mountain and the last rust of evening faded to night. I'd only just opened the door when he thrust his hand inside a brown paper bag and ripped forth a beer, held it to my face. I took the bottle in my hands and then, with a perfect smile, went to close the door; Spike saw it coming and moved fast, slipping a cool boot inside. We struggled a moment, grunting like perverts until finally Spike pried himself through, laughing that lonesome laugh of his as he shuffled inside.

There wasn't so much talk as you might've expected between two friends who hadn't seen each other in coming on a month: the TV chattered on, but other than this there was silence. Not an uncomfortable silence, like the initial hesitation with Aunt Joyce the night before, but only a broken pressure, an idleness that dulled any sense of urgency. I offered him some leftovers of Herring House fries—he was good, thanks—then tossed the beers in the fridge and grabbed a seat. Spike had dropped to his knees and busied himself rolling a joint.

Only after it was done and he was puffing away did Spike open up, starting with how he'd almost been run down by an eighteen-wheeler on the way over, prettiest Peterbilt he'd ever seen, followed by a detailed report of who had been arrested and why. Usual fist-and-knife violence, few sloppy drunks. Another attempt by councilman Matt Figaroy to baby-nap his own son. Nice, Matt, real nice. I could see the bumper stickers now: VOTE FIGAROY—A FATHER WHO CARES!

When he was finished, Spike gave me a knowing look and said, "So been doing a little shopping, have you?"

"Haven't been shopping in years, old pal, you know that."

"I mean *food*, numbskull. I saw you yesterday, in Arapahoe. At the Shop Quick?"

"Arapahoe?" Then it came. "Wait, you mean—the *Datsun?*"

Spike laughed. "Sure, didn't you hear me? Almost crashed a damn lung screaming like that."

"Could've stopped, you know."

"And I would have," he told me, "but Duke was being pissy, said he had to make it out to the harbor by seven."

Of course, I thought. *Duke Spain.*

Duke Spain owned a few of the trawlers down at Fairfield Harbor, but he owned a lot more in the Chesapeake Bay. A whole lot more. And as the reefer made its rounds Spike explained how old Duke had somebody drop out on the *Kimber Faye*, and how Mr. Spain himself had driven all the way to the Bates Motel to personally ask Spike if he'd crowd the saddle. Spike agreed, and later that night, after swallowing most of a bottle of Canadian whisky, he'd fished out Kevin Hillebrandt over at Mulligan's, this tacky beer joint on the shore. Evidently there'd been a good ten minutes of cussing and something nearing a barroom brawl between the time Spike found him and the time he finally walked out. As usual, Spike told the story with grand Gilgamesh-like implications, and when he came to the part about cussing Kevin Hillebrandt he couldn't get out half of what he was saying without one of us cracking up or falling all over the floor. For the first time in a while, Spike actually seemed happy—and more than ready to get out of Reelsboro County.

"So when do you leave?"

"The *Kimber* leaves Friday morning," he said. "And Wes, if you're feeling frisky, you know I could talk to Duke, try and get you a spot on my next boat out—be about two-three weeks. Month caps." He gestured vaguely. "It's up to ya."

"And you can go straight to hell," I told him. "You know how I feel about open water."

Spike raised his hands. "Hey, was only asking. Want anymore?"

I said I didn't and Spike crushed out the joint, then finished his beer and got up to grab another. He called from the kitchen, "So you're doing okay, are you?"

"I'm doing okay."

"Got plenty a biscuits?"

"A few thousand," I said, and then it returned, that vague bearing-down of emotion at the back of my skull, that shrinking at the senselessness and futility of life.

Spike handed me a bottle and plopped to the couch.

"Just a few?"

"Three...maybe four, tops."

"Mm," Spike said, then raised his beer and said, "Well, here's to your health."

"And Prentice? How's he been?"

"Hell, we walked down to Southgate the other night, caught that new Corey Haim flick—"

—"with the vampires?"—

"Yeah, Prentice had been up my ass all week about it, finally went to shut him up. Besides that..." But then something changed, a strained sort of look falling over Spike's face as he stared at his bottle, one finger picking idly at the Budweiser wrapper.

"Wes, do you remember James Harrell?"

And my heart went cold in my chest.

"Stops by every now and again—tall dude, real skinny, walks like Lurch?"

"Sure, I remember," I told him. "Has those funny-looking eyes."

Spike appeared confused, a dull wonder that faded slowly to bewilderment as he shook his head and said, "Wes, lemme tell ya...the other night Prentice beat him to a breath of his life. I mean, I thought the boy was *dead*."

"But *why?*" Staying calm, staying cool. "Why did he do that for?"

"Something about some grass he'd got from Prentice, or some grass he was *supposed* to have got from Prentice. I don't know. One minute the band's up there jamming—just practicing, you know—and next thing here comes James busting through the door, screaming, raising all kinds of hell. So Prentice, he just reaches down and grabs up this bottle, pitches it right at him."

"You're kidding."

"Well, of course it smacks Harrell right in the face—*POW!*—and he hits the floor, blood gushing all over. And now Jamie's crying." I waited as Spike ad-libbed the necessary David Lee Roth vocals. "Next thing, I look and Prentice has jumped off the stage—*flew* off the stage really—and then everybody's clapping along while he..." Spike stared at the floor, and in the dullness of the kitchen lights his face looked weary and streaked and worn. "He whipped him good."

My brain struggled to breathe, to take in and grasp the things I'd heard.

But it was impossible.

"Who else was there?"

Spike thought about it. "Neil was there, Sambo, Antoine's little brother. A couple girls, most of them were asleep. When it was over, Rick and some a Sambo's boys carried him down to the Yard, Tony Donuts called an ambulance. A blue boy came up to the house—was that young fella, Longsmund or Lunsmund—you could tell he was all out of breath from walking up."

"What did he say?"

"Not much. Looked official and asked a bunch of questions. Kinda poked his head in and looked around, but they'd moved a couch over all the blood and cleaned up the rest with some of those old fig-linen sheets. Nobody said a word, and probably James is too scared to say anything— you know James, he'll say it was a wild boar in heat before Prentice comes outta his mouth." He laughed. "Lunsmund sure gave those girls a good scare though—they went to pissin' panties, went out back and hid in the bushes till after he'd gone. Runaways probably."

As he spoke, my body seemed to be sinking lower and lower in the chair. An ash reached ridiculously from the end of my cigarette, defying gravity; I reached over and tapped it in the tray.

"What's going on with him? He strung out?"

"No more than the usual." Spike let out a breath, half-annoyed, half-angry. "Ah, the boy's just gone nuts, Wes, totally flipped his fuckin' wig. All's he talks about anymore is gettin' a motorcycle, which is the *last* thing Prentice needs—boy don't need a car, much less a *cycle*." He sat up suddenly, eyeing his watch. "And here I told that little crackhead I'd be up there tonight..." Spike looked at me, smiling that furtive grin I'd come to know so well over the years. "Wanna come?"

"Honestly...I can't think of anything I'd like less."

Spike laughed and stood to his feet, propping his bottle next to mine on the coffee table.

"Listen, bud, I know you're having your moment and all—and we all have our moments—but your cousin could damn sure use you out there. He's dying, you know. Besides, it ain't healthy being cooped up in here all the time."

"Please don't say that."

"Look," he said, "I leave day after tomorrow. We'll be out for at least two weeks, maybe three, going up as far as New Bedford, maybe even Capeside. So...whatdya say about tomorrow night? We're hitting up Ernul's at eight. R.S.V.P.," he joked, "*invitation only.*"

I realized what he was doing, that Spike was coaxing me not just to come out tomorrow night, but to abandon the comforts of my barbed-wire shell; it was safe in there, after all, potent with a feeling of the known, the controlled. And yet there was a part of me, an altogether darker, wildly suicidal part that now understood Prentice completely, knew intimately his need to fly out of this earth in a tragic blaze of glory, one that left everybody burnt.

It was a feeling that seemed instantly addictive.

"Fine, all right," I told him. "I'll be there. And hey." I walked to the kitchen, retrieving a book from beneath the stack of empty beer cartons. I checked to make sure the envelope hadn't fallen out. "I need you to give this to Prentice."

Spike took the book and held it curiously, as if he'd never seen such a thing, then lifted it to his nose, pulling a deep breath as he flipped the pages.

"Aunt Joyce stopped by," I explained.

"Who?"

"Prentice's mom."

"That right? What'd she want?"

I considered for a moment. "I don't know. Guess she was worried about Prentice." *And I guess she was right*, I thought but didn't say. *What do they call that, mother's intuition?*

Spike nodded, tucking the book under his jacket.

"That's not something she needs to make a habit of doing. Only end up hurting herself, doing something like that." He'd started out when he turned back and said, "And Wes? Get some sleep. Eight o'clock comes early."

Then he stepped out the door and was gone.

§

He was back again the next day, this time minus the beer.

"Figured we might as well walk together," he told me.

So we did, and strolling the roads like old times it occurred to me how close I'd grown to Spike over the last few years; if Prentice was like a brother, then Spike was our resident guardian—an older, wiser child who knew our afflictions well but who always seemed to stay at least head above water, never sinking to the depths Prentice and I were so capable of.

Watching him from the corner of my eye, snakeskin boots pounding the pavement as we walked, I thought back to the first time we'd met; back when I was still the new kid in town and Prentice had brought him over so we could all get stoned and play cards. What happened later is what I remember most, however, when Spike's eyes suddenly slipped shut, head tilting majestically as he began speak-singing the words to "The Gambler." On impulse, Prentice grabbed my old Harmony acoustic and somehow began working accompaniment from its five available strings. Nowadays, on those sleepless mornings, it's not the weekend shows or all the chicks and pills that come back to me: it's that night in my old house, Prentice strumming a ruined guitar as Spike sang with closed eyes, pouring every ounce of his soul into a Kenny Rogers classic.

We stopped to burn a roach behind Ms. Elsa's

shed, afterwards cutting through the soy fields to Oyster Boulevard and down the street to Ernul's. Then I walked through the door and it was as if I'd traveled back in time: local strangers moved from one end of the bar to the other, only this time I knew they were running to nowhere, doing nothing. A small crowd spilled chopped choruses of laughter from the stools, but all I heard were cries for anything but a normal life. There was mirth and smoke and lots of strong smells, but if you watched carefully from where I stood you could see the faded faces of the men and women who had come before—long, sad, murdered by the thing they feared the most: a dry life that ended as pointlessly as it had been carried out.

The only thing that really seemed to have changed was me.

We grabbed some beers and settled in our booth and soon Spike was in another world, eyes heavy-lidded and lips soothing to some Bob Seger tune coming down in mono; I sensed his mind moving back and forth in time, maybe dreaming of restless waves and long nights and the fragmented reality of life on the boat. The latest from Springsteen was met with a row of applause as I noticed a familiar shadow past the stained glass of the door; then the door opened and the darkness slithered inside, a few dead leaves scuttling in at his feet.

He wore a sort of trench coat, actually more of a duster—some black thing that hung as loosely around his body as it would have a coat hanger;

fat violet bags festered beneath his eyes. Everyone turned, watching with shy curiosity as he started across the floor, and in that moment I believed I would actually witness a miracle; that here in this paltry bar Prentice would simply fade into nothingness, be gone, and vanish.

I waited for the rest of the band to follow him inside, but they never did. He was alone, and something told me this was his natural habitat; oh sure, he'd plenty of fair-weather friends and women, and people came from all around to sit with his sullen assembly, but make no mistake—Prentice was separated. Separated from me, though we were brothers; separated from Spike, though it was him who'd seen Prentice through that gray area of boy-to-man; and, most of all, I believe he was separated from himself...

"*Wes!*" he gushed. "I've missed you, honey-child, where you been hidin'?"

"Well," Spike muttered, "if it ain't Evel Knievel himself."

"Biggest rock I could find," I said, sliding to make room in the booth.

He gave me a funny smile. "Been dangling from them gallows again, huh?"

I'd started a glance to my hand, stopping myself at the last second. Not that it mattered; the last of the scab I'd picked off the night before, exposing the tender, pig-belly pink flesh beneath. I returned the smile, not so sure my vise-grip wouldn't crack the bottle in one hand.

"Welcome back, old man," he said, clapping my shoulder and climbing into the booth. "Merry-go-round hasn't been the same without ya."

"And I came for what—*for this?* To look at your ugly face and realize I'm your cousin and *hope and pray* it doesn't run in the family? Or maybe catch some dick-rot disease from one of these free-wheelin' floaters? Just thinking about it, I hate myself and wish I was dead." I'd meant it as a joke, but just then everything got quiet and my face was on fire.

"I'll tell you what's dead," Spike said, scoping out the bar. "*This* place is dead, even for a Thursday..."

"They're probably out there already," Prentice said, eyes staring darkly into space. "Waiting for me to swoop down and sing them to sleep, like some lullaby jukebox everybody can lean on when they've had a bad life. Pop in a quarter, toss back a beer, suddenly I've got half the town breathing down my neck and making last minute offers for an encore. I don't think so." Prentice snatched up a bottle, looked at me. "They're leeches, Wes: idiot savants, beggars of bread, if you know what I mean. And I'm about sick and tired of 'em picking the crumbs off *my* lips. But that's all right. Just wait till I get my bike, think it's about time I start sucking some blood myself..."

Spike gave me a look—*do you see?*—as Prentice jammed the neck of his beer against the table, giving it a knock. And while I didn't know what had put this new chip on Prentice's shoulder, I *could* see what Spike was talking about: the boy really had gone crazy. I couldn't put my finger on it, exactly, on just *how* he seemed so different, or what it was that made even his smile seem ugly, but gone was the presence of something like awe for him—and in its place stood a wicked emotion, like passing some gory interstate pileup. He knew it too; maybe it was the sudden flashes of sadness in his eyes, or the way he carried himself just a little too surely, like a kid Icarus who hasn't quite realized those wings are made of wax.

As the endless chatter of the bar crept slowly back into mind, I looked up and Prentice was staring at me. He smiled darkly before turning to Spike, who had been rattling on about the seventies and about wild cocaine parties on the boat—the binge of '81, for instance—and of great whore orgies at sea. Staring past his cigarette, Spike went on to describe The Big Score on Cape May, followed by the seven-car pileup on the drive back from Jersey. With one finger he drew a long scar down his shoulder blade and stopped suddenly, head drooping as his eyes met mine in quick apology.

Only after a few more rounds did I notice the stranger at the end of the bar.

Smaller, well-dressed, only his faded leather jacket seeming out of place. As I watched, he knocked back the last of his drink before starting casually over, and only then did I realize just why this man seemed so familiar...

Spike saw it and turned, watching as the stranger approached the table and smiled his innocent virgin smile. "Ray Lafargue," he said, "if it isn't my favorite French-lipped gigolo. Still rocking the leather after all these years?"

But Ray only grinned. "And how's my favorite gypsy carpenter, eh? You know, I hear Kevin Hillebrandt is in need of some good help—I could give him a ring, if you're interested..."

Spike reached out, serving a quick-fingered jab to the man's ribs as he moved to make room in the booth. Ray appraised Prentice, who raised an unsteady finger and said, "Wait, sure, I know this cat here, right? Met you somewhere before, man..."

"Not that I'm aware of," said Ray, smiling. "I get that a lot, though. The whole town knows who you are, brother. Your voice is incredible."

Prentice gulped the rest of his beer, then let fly with a hairy belch.

"So did you ever get that dredge offer you were waiting for?" Spike asked. "The one you were so *sure* you were gonna get?

Ray adjusted his collar. "Of course I got the offer. Stick Folsom is one greedy, whisker-tweaking landlubber, but he's about as ignorant as his head is thick."

No idea what they were talking about.

"Just got back from Louisiana three days ago, been shacking up with Keri Scott ever since. Fellas tell me you're riding out tomorrow morning, figured I might as well come down and bid you right.

And since there's no such thing as sealegs without a hangover..."

He dug deep in the pockets of his crumbled leather jacket, and I half-expected to see his fingers shooting through a hole on the other side. They didn't, and instead he produced a thick wad of cash, spun it casually, and slammed a hot hundred on the table.

"Who's up for another round?"

Hoots, cheers, hollers like fireworks on the Fourth of July, and beyond this the table became a wasteland of smoke and spilled laughter and twice-told tales. Oysters were ordered, and with them I recall Buster slipping us an armful of those little Bacardi one-shots, even though everyone knew what a terrible idea it was as we recited the Drunkard's Creed: *Beer before liquor never been sicker, beer before liquor never been sicker...*

By the time two a.m. rolled around with last call, there was only one fellow remaining survivor left in the bar—some poor geezer slumped over like a corpse, sipping stale Coors from a can. Watching from the corner of my eye, I noticed him trading wearied glances between his watch, us, Buster cutting off lights and tidying things up around the bar, back to his watch again, as if he couldn't quite understand what in the world was *happening.* Finally he stood and shuffled for the door, his worn soles scuffing the floor as if he were already the toilet-papered mummy he would one day become...

§

Afterwards we moved outside, picking our slow and steady way around the corner and over to the old alley next to the bar. The alley was narrow—just north of arm's reach—but had served us well on many of our worst nights, and we were still settling in when suddenly we looked and the old geezer came shuffling toward us in the darkness.

"*Prentice*," he called, stumbling closer. "*Prentice, I just wanted to tell you...how much...I enjoy your music. I really do. I can't tell you what it means to me.*" His voice rattled as he spoke, the folds of his neck quivering softly against the moon. "*Thank you, Prentice. Thank you...*"

We stared in silence as Prentice walked over, embracing the old man's shoulders. Gazing deep within the ore of his bloodshot eyes, Prentice nodded gravely, affected a gentle, heartfelt smile...and then briskly doubled over, spewing vomit all over the man's antique shoes.

The old-timer gasped, turning to flee but not fast enough as Prentice gave chase down the alley, gagging like a zombie and doing his best to shoot projectile vomit at the geezer's tattered flannel jacket. A moment later he lingered back, his face berry with exhaustion.

"*Got him!*" he declared. "With that limp, ol' boy didn't stand much of a chance..."

Prentice flailed wildly, doing his best Fleeing Geezer, and we couldn't help it then and burst into laughter; Spike doubled over, grabbing at the walls, Ray collapsing in sloppy paroxysms to the earth. Moments later he stood, lifting a small pipe from his pocket and fiddling with it, twisting things here and there. He'd pulled a small baggie from his pocket when—

"That won't be necessary," Prentice said, and reaching down proceeded to produce one of the biggest, most lethal bags of weed I've ever witnessed. In a glare of light, I imagined a thin streaking of color down its side, and in my drunken fantasies knew that it was blood. *"This one's on Jamie."*

Crawling out of his duster, he grabbed a few prodigious pinches from the bag and slowly the pipe made its rounds, making pass after silent pass until finally my heart hummed like a motor and the stars came alive and somewhere a bird cawed and everyone smiled because we were stoned, but I knew we were just local strangers.

For a long time we sat in the clumsy silence, Prentice finally hopping to his feet and strolling casually down the alley, stopping beneath the blackened windows of the building next door. Despite the place being abandoned, the windows were covered in ghetto bars, and leaping high Prentice grabbed hold and pulled himself up; for a moment he hung there, spying through the perpetually fogged glass before dropping and tossing a careless finger to the building's side entrance.

"Let's do it...let's go in..."

Not as a question but rather a command, and no sooner had the order been given than Spike scurried absently to his feet; without thinking, I started for the door, only to be cut off by Ray, who tried the knob first one way, then the other.

"Locked," he said.

This is madness, you know.

Prentice mumbled something—*figured as much, is what I think he said*—then bent low and began tightening the laces of his combat boots, both scuffed and dirty.

How much longer do you think something like this can go on, Wes?

Without somebody getting hurt?

He stood now, doing a series of stretches, cracking his neck...

Without death?

"I'm going home."

Prentice glared at me, his face a paler, somehow softer version of itself in the moonlight. It was the only thing soft about him; as a whole, his body was hard and sharp, ribs shrinking and swelling with each raspy breath. His eyes were cold and serious.

"C'mon, Wes..."

At times it was a tricky thing to duck out on my cousin; he was a high roller, after all, self-taught in the school of hard knocks, and to him cutting out was akin to giving up...and he had little pity for the weak of heart. Prentice was one of those guys who crept around at night giving sleepers automatic mohawks or drawing on faces with lipstick. He was the one who blasted the stereo when sleep would've otherwise come easy, or dropped a steamy dump in your tennies and pushed it down into the toes the way middle-aged men hide their wallets at the beach.

But I didn't care.

I wasn't staying, and if I hadn't known it before I realized it now: namely, that I didn't like this Prentice, didn't like this ugly thing he'd become; he was numb and careless and cruel. He made me nervous. I wanted to get away from him.

Only then—that flash of sadness—and he cracked a smile. Just a small one, a mere curling of the lips that in some other world might've been the play of light and shadow on his face—

But it was enough.

"Those gallows again, uh?" He stared, peering at me through eyes that would've had understanding in them if they weren't so black and gone, so far outside of himself.

Slowly, he nodded.

"Go on..."

So I went, hobbling furiously down the alley and then out into the streets, followed in the darkness by the loud, gong-like echoes of Prentice kicking at the door, again and again and again...

LOCAL STRANGERS, CONT.

In the darkness I watched, lone figures dancing wild in the desert around a bright-burning fire. Howling, grunting as overhead the sky swirled in a shifting neon curtain—now black, now red, now blue and green and purple. Then another figure—hunchbacked, covered in hair, eyes burning hellfire red against the night as it soared higher and higher, slowly blotting the stars.

It lunged for me then, arms stretching morbidly through the fire as I turned and fled across the desert, running faster, faster as the breath came warm at my neck and then I felt the long, cold bite and when I opened my eyes I was lying in bed and there was pounding at the door.

I pulled myself up, still catching my breath, and

climbing out of bed it occurred to me it had been over two months since the last time Prentice slept over—and now, of all nights, he came. Probably being funny, I thought, being a double-douche since I'd cut out on him so early. I snatched open the door, half-expecting somebody to do me a favor and blow off a piece of my head, spraying a nice tint of red and skull-tone over the finer works of Salvador Dalí.

But they didn't. Instead there was only the rain, a heavy one I hadn't noticed until now. The screen door fluttered softly against the wind, and only after a moment did I notice the small shadow at the end of the porch; he stepped forward, clothes dripping as he ran one wearied hand down his face.

"Hello, Weston," he said, the sleeve of his crumbled leather jacket grazing my arm as he brushed past me into the house.

"You're soaked," I told him, not feeling all that great suddenly, and went to grab a towel from the hall closet. When I came back, Ray had stripped from his jacket and was pawing the rain from his hair. I handed off the towel and, before I could beat him to it, he sank into my chair. So I just sort of flopped to the couch and let out a nice wide yawn, playing it up for effect.

"You alone?"

"Well, Spike left not long after you," he said. "And Prentice...last I saw Prentice, he was sawing logs in that old crypt next to the bar. It was absolutely freezing in there, Wes, just terrible..."

"Sure he wasn't dead?"

Ray laughed and lit a cigar from his pocket, puffing away. "Can you believe, this is the first cigar I've had in over eight years? The last was better, of course, but then it was Cuban. Have you ever had a Cuban? The Cubans make excellent cigars. That Vuelta Abajo blend, there's nothing like it in the world; oh, but that goes back to the 1800's. I've been to a factory once, you know, in Cuba—the way their hands moved! And their eyes—there was *passion* in those eyes, Wes. I had a passion once. Did you ever have a passion?"

I sat back on the couch, still yawning. "Sleep."

Ray laughed and said, "Here, maybe this will help." He tossed over the bag he'd offered Prentice hours earlier.

"Need a pipe?"

I told him I didn't and fetched my bowl, and beyond this found I didn't much care what Ray said. All I knew was I couldn't suffer through any more of his mindless soul chatter without either getting high or systematically banging all hell out of my fingers with a mallet. Ray picked up where he'd left off as I loaded the bowl, going on about how he'd moved from everywhere to back again when he was a kid, and how his dad was this real Navy prick and his parents never let him have friends because they moved so much and *bluh bluh bluh*...

And I just sat there and sort of nodded and coughed, tried to be a little shoulder, you know. Still sort of wondering what he was doing here and what I thought I could do about it. Only then he'd started in about running away to 'Frisco and I noticed something change in his voice.

"I was young then," he said. "Things were different in those days, there was something in the air—my parents just didn't know it. Can you blame them? They were raised in a different world. Did you know, they wouldn't let me watch the Beatles on Ed Sullivan? Nope. Haircuts every three weeks—buzzed, of course. So one night I'd had enough and just walked out, walked right out the house and started down the road and I never looked back. I was picked up three days later, fifty miles from the Haight—so close, Wes, so close I could *taste* the freedom..."

I was still sort of staring at the crazy look in his eyes when Ray leaned slowly forward and said, "I know what's happened with your cousin, Weston."

I just nodded at him sagely, not really meaning it.

"What's happened with him?"

Ray smiled. "Prentice is a strange cat, Weston. He's *brilliant*, actually. I'm not brilliant. I only know because it happened to me."

"Ah?"

"Like I said, they sent me away to the loony bin for that little trip to 'Frisco. *Want to act crazy,* they said, *then fine. Go wild.* Oh, there were all sorts in that place: mad priests and addicts, tree porkers and runaways and vets. Delinquents, kleptos, pyros, all of us thrown together in some crazy stew. But one night I was in bed, just looking out over the sky through those little windows they had, looking up at the moon and all the little tops of the trees. And almost like he knew exactly what I was thinking, like he could *feel* me in the darkness, the guy in the next bed turns and starts talking to me. He'd never looked so young as he did that night, Wes, with the moon on him like that."

A subtle sort of melancholy had fallen over his face.

"We talked and I told him about my passion—to experience all that life had to offer, no holding back—and he just laughed and looked at the ceiling. I asked him why he was in there, and he told me that's where he belonged. Said he'd committed himself—not because he was crazy but because he was *sent*, because he knew there were people there who needed him. Maybe even people like me. He'd had a passion once, too—and he'd got what he wanted. Told me if I wanted it bad enough, I could get mine the same way. And he told me how. I was only sixteen years old. That was 1967."

I couldn't help it then, and laughed.

"*Nineteen sixty-seven*, Ray? C'mon—that's twenty years ago."

"Hard to believe..."

I sensed my patience fading, fast. Being too stoned made that feeling worse, somehow, scarier than it should've been; too many walls, no way out. "Bullshit, that'd make you like...you'd be like a *forty-year-old*."

"Thirty-six."

"Yeah. Thirty-six."

Ray reached around and opened his wallet, handed me a card. "See for yourself."

So I took the card, looked it over—and promptly assured him it was a fake. Had seen a million just like it.

"No, it's legit," he said mildly. "You could cut me in half and count the rings if you wanted, but I really don't care if you believe me or not."

Far from forty, with his baby face and perfect skin Ray looked even younger than Spike, who only last February had celebrated the big three-oh.

"It's not right," I told him. "Can't be."

"I take care of myself, Weston. Try to anyway."

I gave back his card, grateful to get the filthy thing out of my hands. There were a lot of things I could've said to him then, but I stuck with the one that mattered.

"What does any of this have to do with Prentice?"

"That man was right, Wes. I wanted to see the world, wanted to *taste* it—if only once before I died. That next morning he was gone, never to be heard from again. But something happened after I got out of that place. I had a dream about a walk beside the water, and in the dream I met with something that knew what I wanted and who I knew could give it to me. And true to that man's word, they did. Only there's a high price for such things, and I was willing to pay it—so I did."

Ray took a deep breath, fear for the first time bubbling beneath his words.

"Twenty years can't separate what happened, and neither can death. But as long as I'm here, I still have a passion—they can never take that away. Only the passion died a long time ago and now I'm just...running from the inevitable." A slow tear slipped down his cheek as the kitchen lights flickered softly behind him. He smiled pathetically and said, "When I woke up, I found this."

Ray slowly popped the buttons down his shirt and pulled it aside, revealing a tangled mass of folds and tissue over the flesh of his chest.

"This is my surrender, Weston: this is everything I hoped for and everything I have to show for it. This is all I'll ever know. See how thick it is? Look at it sideways—see how it looks like a kiss? See the purple lipstick?" Ray replaced his collar and said, "Wes...tonight I saw this same mark on your cousin."

Slam.

Crash.

I looked at him, not wanting to understand but getting it just the same. "What are you saying? That Prentice is...is what?"

"I'm trying to say that Prentice gave himself to the same thing I did, and that he's killing himself because of it."

"That he's *evil? Possessed?*"

"That he's too smart for his own good, more like. I've *accepted* what I've done, and now I live every day on purpose because I know that's all I can do. I'm running, Prentice is running—we're all *running*, but at least I know that I'm running and I'm doing it because I care. It's my fate."

I sprang forward, leaping from the couch as I allowed the fury to take hold, letting it make me one with its perfect wild-eyed hunger. "You're out of your fucking head, man…" I was sort of pacing. "I mean it, you're over the fucking *rainbow*. Prentice ain't like us, he could have a hundred scars, a thousand—*so what?*"

"Prentice is a lot like us, especially me. And a hundred scars are fine as long as not one of them looks like a big pair of lips on top of his heart. Then again, maybe somebody *did* stab him in the chest with a machete. Maybe he *did* run straightway into a chainsaw. Maybe somebody *did* jam his nipple in a blender. Don't believe me? Go see for yourself. It's real, Wes—*I know*. Just like I know all about what happened to your hand."

"Get out."

"I was there," he said, "followed you all the way home, right through the woods. Or how'd you think I found the place? You ran through the streets like a stuck pig."

With a quickness that surprised even me, I walked over and threw back the door; the crash of rain came spilling inside.

"You need to go now, Ray."

"Listen, I came here to help," he said, standing calmly to his feet. "We can help him, I know we can. There are things out there that just aren't known—things beyond this physical world. Unseen things. Things I've experienced. Wes, I know shit you can't read about in some book, seen shit you wouldn't believe. It's not over for him, not if you don't want it to be. He doesn't have to keep running like I do..."

But by then I'd had enough—enough of the games, enough of everything. I told him to get out, not in the nicest way, and like a well-minded dog Ray scooped up his jacket and slumped to the door.

And stopped.

"I wouldn't mention any of this to Prentice, by the way." He glanced back, eyes still puppy-dogging with sorrows and regret. "You know he's gonna say you're crazy either way..."

He turned to leave and finally I saw my shot, serving a hard kick to the ass that sent Ray sprawling off the porch, followed by a deep splatter as he landed in the mud. As the rain fell splashing around him, I cackled wildly and then slammed the door, conscious suddenly of the all-over numbness of my fingers.

My hands were shaking.

§

Later that night, caught somewhere in that dubious half-realm between waking and sleep, I decided I had to see it. If it was real—if there really was any scar—and if it had anything to do with what was happening to Prentice, I wanted to know.

I had to see it for myself.

II: BROKEN SLEEP

YELLA HOUSE

When it came to mornings in Reelsboro County, the Herring House had long been established as the only place that mattered: family-owned and operated since 1918, founded on grease-heavy southern cooking and spanning now three generations of Reelsboro-bred breakfast royalty, the House was a tradition that seemed sure to last. The only thing missing here was a giant sign in the window out front: THE HERRING HOUSE—EXPANDING WAISTLINES FOR OVER SIXTY UNFORGETTABLE YEARS!!!

Pushing through the door, I was immediately overwhelmed with the smell of coffee and Seafood Benedict, slightly burned toast, still-cooking cheddar browns. A line of customers jagged from the register at the front, most glaring ravenously at the large blue-lettered menu strung up over the counter. I stepped in behind a man who smelled strangely like a burlap sack, waiting there until the kid behind the counter recognized me as Prentice's cousin and took me aside, scribbling down my order. I poured some coffee from the setup along the wall—always black before nine, and it was right at quarter of—and grabbed a seat at an empty table near the window.

The ding of the cash register as someone paid, more tingling of a bell and someone shuffled into line.

Outside people hurried past, scurrying over the sidewalk and smiling at the sky, remarking on what a lovely weekend it would be and how they should probably take out the boat, maybe do a little work in the garden. A trip to the park. Watching them my mind turned to Prentice, to the night before in the alley and the loud gong of his boot as it struck the door over...and over...and over. Had I really walked away? Just like that? Yes, I really had. It occurred to me that it was still early, and if Prentice had actually crashed in that building next to the bar—unlikely—then maybe he was still there. Why, if one were so inclined to ask, he may even break off a nice little snack from that lethal bag of grass...

I slurped at my coffee, turning things over and over in my head until at last I could stand it no longer and rose to my feet, walking out the door and joining the masses on their endless march to nowhere.

I strolled down Madam Moore's Lane, maple trees glowing bright in the sun as blackbirds and cardinals stirred in the branches overhead, small messengers of black and red. Approaching Ernul's, I noticed Prentice's leftovers from late the night before, stale puddles of vomit spotting obscenely across the pavement. Then came a subtle peace as I entered the alley—a very rational, very reasonable voice speaking only in the calm tongues of sanity: Prentice would take the stage sometime after nine, Spike was somewhere off skating the coast, and all was right with the world. For a moment it seemed as if everything up to that point in my life had been only a dream, some strange existence from which I'd finally woken. It was a nice thought.

Fleeting, but nice.

They'd done a number on the door—the hinges were partway snapped—and moving inside, massive stilts of steel appeared from the darkness, running from floor to unseen ceiling. My foot brushed over something on the floor, and looking I saw what appeared to be the remains of a half-burned shirt—Prentice's, I think—then turned to see a figure shuffling toward me in the darkness.

He mumbled my name and said something about browning out his trousers, said he didn't think he'd be seeing me here this early, just what the hell did I think I was doing? Prentice shivered as he spoke, voice raspy and dry.

He seemed sober.

"Got an order in at the House," I told him, trying for casual. "You?"

"Just waiting on Buster," he told me, groaning as he stretched beneath the crackling flaps of his duster. "You know me, gotta have a drink to get rid of the hangover."

Ernul's didn't open for another couple of hours, but most afternoons Buster came in early to watch the comedians on TV, and he'd usually let us hang out as long as we weren't being too obnoxious.

We stood for a moment in silence, soaking in the darkness until finally Prentice dragged a hand down his face and stumbled for the door.

"C'mon," he said. "I'll walk ya back."

Prentice struck a smoke as we wandered outside, and in this new light of morning I noticed drying streaks of blood running from his nostrils; he wiped them casually away and squinted into the distance, spreading the tattered flaps of his duster and then pulling them closed. He stifled a yawn and said, "Had another dream last night..."

And a large ball of spit went rolling down the back of my throat.

"Oh yeah? Any naked ladies?"

No naked ladies, he said, laughing, and told me it had something to do with the band. Said in the dream they'd had all-new instruments and were set up in this huge open-air stadium, stars twinkling overhead. Prentice's hand swept vaguely across the sky and he was about to say more when he stopped suddenly, one arm reaching out and pulling me close to a weave basket currently on display in a thrift store window.

"Don't look now," he said, and looking I saw a man in dark sunglasses and a Leif Garret bandana strolling blithely across the street. Prentice whispered something; it sounded like long johns.

"Huh?"

"*Long John!*" he hissed. "*The one with the lingerie...*"

I pressed my face to the glass, staring beyond the basket to a forgotten heaven of tarnished jewels: miniature tea sets and record players and golf clubs. Up front an old woman sat hunched behind her table, a sign overhead declaring I BREAK I CRY, YOU BREAK YOU BUY. Slowly the man moved past behind our backs, then dipped around a corner and out of sight. We started walking.

"He, uh, still write you those poems?"

"Not in a while, no. And they weren't *poems*, they were more like—" Prentice shook it off, got back on track. "*Anyway*, point is, we were all set up in this cool-ass stadium and tuned up and ready to go, were gonna open with 'Cockatrice Djinn,'— you know, *The man with the plan in a tall black suit...*"

We sang the next lines together: "*The face with a taste for a small southern town...everywhere and nowhere and all around...*"

"And then..." Prentice dragged hard from his cigarette, blew it out. "And then, I dunno, something changed. The crowd got louder and louder but...but it's like they weren't even *cheering* anymore, sounded like they were *dying* out there..."

I looked at him then, and although he'd never admit it—and of course I'd never ask him to—I believe I saw fear in those dark eyes, maybe for the first time. But no sooner had I picked it out, no sooner had the terror surfaced than the blinds promptly dropped, whatever fears I'd imagined vanishing from his face.

"Here's the real kicker, though," he told me, and at these words his duster flapped back, my stomach lurching as the scar shone bright in the morning sun: a ghastly, purpled mass of tissue rising from the flesh just over his heart. I stared blindly, wondering after its meaning and implications and all of it rushing back as I glanced up and saw him staring at me with those faded eager eyes.

"I look around, and realize I'm seeing all this from *behind the drums*."

"Wow."

"*I was the fuckin' DRUMMER.*"

Prentice choked another drag from his cigarette, and without wanting to I saw the scar—no bigger than Ray's, but with that same lipstick sheen—swell and rise over his chest, and immediately wished I'd never seen it, never made the walk this morning, never stepped foot outside the door.

"What do you think it means?" I asked, struggling to gather the pieces of everything we'd been talking about before, before, before.

Prentice only shrugged. "Maybe there should be some change, a new drummer. I mean, I love Olympus the way it is, I *love* this fuckin' band. And I love Rick, we've had some good times, but lately, I don't know..." Prentice smirked, shaking his head. "Who knows? Maybe it means I should burn down the house...kill a man...rob a bank..."

His voice rambled out ahead of me, numbering off dastardly deeds (*shave my head, go preggers, join a cult*), until finally I could stand it no longer, couldn't possibly go on holding it in because over my shoulder was another voice—this one of Ray, his cryptic diatribe wheezing in my ear, egging me on—and without thinking I aimed a finger to his chest and said, "Looks like you got some shrapnel from the war."

Prentice glanced down, a nonplussed expression dawning over his face as he took the meat of the scar between his fingers, gave it a squeeze. "Now *that*," he said, "that is all-over nasty. Must've hurt, for sure."

"How'd it happen?"

"Hm." He gave it another squeeze. "I don't think I could tell ya, Wes. Probably one night sometime..."

"You mean...you don't even *remember?*"

Prentice shook his head, no big deal, drawing a final puff from his cigarette and thumping it away. In a daze, I watched as it rolled to some faraway drain to be forgotten. He glanced up the street and said, "Since I'm already down this far, think

I'll walk over to Quincy Jay's, maybe check out this bike he's been talking about. Supposed to give me a good deal..."

It's a surreal feeling to look back and know that moment when life takes a turn that, once made, is forever unalterable. It wasn't just Ray's visit the night before, though that had a lot to do with it; it was walking down the street that morning of late August '87 and realizing your best friend—not only that, your very own blood—was the one to tell you that life is existence in a hidden closet. That there are no companions on that long, hard road, only temporary shoulders to lean on while you each catch your breath. My mind fought back the notion, resisting its treacherous insinuations—but I knew. Oh, I knew.

I knew because he was lying.

"Are you playing tonight?"

"I suppose," he said, "if the notion strikes me. I'm sure it's struck everyone else..."

"I talked to your mom."

"Oh yeah?"

"Yeah. Did Spike give you the book?"

"You're right." He fished an envelope from his pocket, ripped it open. "I don't know anything about no book, though. What kinda book?"

Hesitantly: "Looked like a...book about God?"

Prentice brayed laughter. "At least she's original. Was she worried about me? Crying?"

I nodded.

Prentice grabbed some money from the envelope, flipping the pages of a letter back and forth. He stuffed the bills in his pocket; the letter he balled up and tossed in the street.

He said, "She's gonna get a headache, she keeps that up."

"She said your dad got saved."

This time the laughter was louder, scoffing. "My dad ain't got *saved*—probably hoofed some powder and thought he touched the face of God. Hell, I'll bet James Harrell thought he tweaked His mustache." He glanced at me from the side of his face. "Spike tell you?"

"Yeah, he told me."

"Blood just don't move like that, not that I've ever seen." Prentice beamed unabashedly. "It was great."

A moment of silence passed, the Herring House looming bright yellow on the horizon.

I asked, "Why?"

Prentice looked at me, then shook his head: "*James is an idiot.*"

He threw back his hair, laughing with the pride and reckless abandon usually charged to youth as rebellion but which I imagined was something else: a new person, new nature. I was aware of some new presence in Prentice—one of despair, of terror and destruction—and I didn't like it, not even a little bit. It made me nervous.

For the second time in twenty-four hours, I wanted to get away from him.

Approaching the Herring House door, Prentice lit another smoke as we made plans to see each other later that night. And though he never offered a pinch of grass from his bag or any surprising vial of pills, at the time it was the farthest thing from my mind.

That would come later.

Now I just needed space, lots of space, and was reaching for the door when I felt the cold touch of his hand on my shoulder.

"Let me ask you something," he said. "You ever read about dreams? I know you have, you gave me all them books about that. But...what do you think it means? My dream?" Prentice glared at me from behind his cigarette, a subtle sincerity making him offer up the words. "I mean, if you had to bet?"

"Me?" I looked him in the eyes and shook my head. "I don't think it means anything. Just a dream, Prentice. That's all."

It was the first time I had lied to my cousin in a long, long time.

Or felt the need to.

§

Sometimes people make decisions they shouldn't make.

They do things they shouldn't be doing and everybody knows it but them, everybody can see it moving and changing them, turning them. You want to protect them, sometimes you just wanna roll up your sleeves and beat the sense into them if you could—but you *can't*, it's not something you fight like that. In the end, you can only stand back and watch as they fade into these shadows that move slower and slower until one day they stop moving at all and you let out this long breath that has in it the power to fog a thousand windows.

Life is like that sometimes.

I walked home and fell on the couch, hoping to forget the whole business if only for a little while, knowing it was impossible. My mind wouldn't quit, still reeling from the curse hidden in plain sight across my cousin's chest and knowing that forever after, in the most mundane of happenings, in the smallest details, there would always be more than meets the eye. All of it cycling back to Ray and his gloomy voice in my ear, not much different than the night before but only seen in a different light.

I was there...

How'd ya think I found the place?

You ran through the streets like a stuck pig...

This followed by another memory, back to when I was twelve and had come to spend the weekend with Prentice and his family. I kept thinking about Uncle Fred, and how he'd been fussing about all those bees ruining the wood in his garage. About how Prentice and I had spent all afternoon swatting the things with tennis rackets, even got two dollars apiece for doing it; Uncle Fred had smiled indulgently and said, "You've earned it boys," and told me I needed to come around more often, with an arm like that. Then he'd tousled our hair and walked back inside.

But mostly I thought of Ray (*we can help him*

you know), conjuring images of the unholy surgery across his heart; only now it was Prentice's heart, dark and horrible in the smoky chamber of his chest. Then flashes of other scars—first my hand, then another, much uglier scar trailing down my—

I leapt to my feet, pacing now as I fought back nerves and fears and the down-deep feeling that I was falling from a high, high place. I went over and retched into the sink, pausing long enough to wash it down before walking out the door.

MULLIGAN'S

The rosy smell of crabs lay thick in the wind as the old tavern appeared up ahead, oddly sinister against the shore. As far as bars go, Mulligan's was a nice one. They didn't have a menu—part of the reason Ernul's suffered the riff-raff it did—but Mulligan's did offer cleaner faces with prettier smiles and tables that didn't move more like rocking chairs. Best of all it was on the waterfront, and standing outside one could stare serenely over and without squinting observe the glory of Fairfield Harbor, with its long docks and warehouses and spidery-looking ships.

I'd walked this way a handful of times since moving to Reelsboro, mostly on a lark: a day trip to waste away the time. Today offered no such luxury, however, and in the five hours since leaving home I'd trekked the Norfolk Southern line through the woods to Arapahoe and all the way to the shore. Here the Marsten Road swept past the harbor, offering a scenic if shit-smelly tour past Mulligan's and into Trent Woods and finally on out of Reelsboro County...if one were so inclined.

I mounted the bar's wraparound porch, knees knocking around like a pair of cymbals as I looked around and saw sailboats and trawlers cruising dream-like across the waters of the Sound. Approaching the front doors, I spotted two old-timers in rocking chairs at the end of the porch, each pausing long enough to stare before gulping from their beers. *"Doors don't open 'nother two hours,"* I heard one of them say, and kept walking as if I hadn't.

I tried the double doors and walked inside, "Cherry Bomb" by John Mellencamp blaring from a nearby jukebox. The place was gutted except for a group at one end of the bar—four or five guys of dirtied clothes and a rank fish smell—but I could sense the ghosts everywhere, a subtle film that sopped the walls and fell in slow-moving waves over the windows. I walked to the bar and glanced around, eyes sliding over the pool tables and the flashing juke, the sturdy wooden tables with checked oilcloths.

The bartender spotted me and walked over.

"Can I do for you?" he asked.

"I need to know where Keri Scott lives."

The boys at the end let out a row of giggles; the bartender cut eyes in their direction and they turned away, quiet despite the soft jumps of their shoulders.

"Now is that right? And you wouldn't be that deadbeat she's gone on about—the *bum*, yeah? Real sweet-talker?"

Dead stare. A sharp pain from my knees.

"Or you just another flyboy motherfucker, one more maggot come to—hey, don't you think she's been through *enough* already? Enough without all this? I'm gonna tell you like I told the last guy, which is I think the best thing for—"

"*Look*," I snapped, "I don't even *know* Keri Scott ya old bat, I'm just lookin' for Ray, that's all I'm tryna do. He said he was *stayin'* with the woman."

Only then I remembered the rhyme, the childish beat of it floating out of memory and sing-songing into my head: *Scot-Free Keri Scott, She'll Give You What She's Got, She Don't Need A Lot, 'Cuz She Don't WANNA Stop, Scot-Free Keri Scott...*

The bartender looked at me, somewhat appeased, still suspicious.

"You one a Ray's buddies?" he asked, and I told him no, that I was making the whole thing up. I could feel the eyes of the men at the end of the bar. "Listen," he said, "I've known Keri a long time, like she's my own. Now I've seen some bad things in my day—but lemme warn ya, I could do a lot worse, somebody turned me right and made me..."

I jumped up, sort of muttering as I stole away from the counter and back toward the door. I would slam it—*hard*—hopefully shattering the glass, and with the pieces I would stand before them and mutilate myself all over their clean little floor, carving bleak meaningless messages into my chest and arms. Yeah, that'd teach 'em. That'd show 'em how—

"Wait," the man called. "Now just *wait.*"

I turned back, glaring at the old bastard. If he shot off at the mouth with another round of that sheep dip I thought I'd break one of his bones— the shin, maybe. *I'm ready, you wanna throw? I'll get down you sagged old miser, when I get done you'll be doing damage control on your prostate...*

One of the men stood from his stool at the end of the bar.

The bartender bent over, leaning at me with his endless shoulders. His voice was lower now.

"If you're looking for Ray...Keri lives just up the road a bit, quarter-mile pushin'. You pass the woods between here and there—" he pointed to somewhere beyond the walls. "Just follow the Marsten Road. An old blue single-wide just on the other side, hole in the wall size of a Mack truck." He muttered something about a hurricane and twitched his head. "One with the kiddie junk strewn all over the...well, you'll see the dog. Name a Dozer."

"*Dozer?* As in 'He Who Sleeps' Dozer?"

Click of his throat. "As in Bull Dozer. Big Mastiff."

The bartender smiled weakly, tipped his head as if making a bow, and stumbled away. He grabbed a towel from a cluttered shelf of whiskey, started polishing at shines on the counter. The men at the far side had resumed their conversation.

I turned and was walking out the door when I heard the sound of the bartender's voice calling after me: *"If you pass the water tower you've gone too far..."*

Only then his voice was gone, swallowed by the squeal of the door and the slow crash of waves over the shore. The old-timers laughed from their post, still felled in their ancient rockers. One wrinkled face turned to glare at me down the porch.

§

I found the trailer just off the main road.

The foundation was off, I could tell—the east end swung out a little—and coming closer I noticed the sheet of plastic over the far side, saw the plywood beneath covering a hole the size of a mammoth's fist. Not far beyond the trailer, the waves beat at the shore with their constant ebb and flow, a soothing *swoosh* through the trees.

The bartender was right: the front yard existed in a clutter of time-worn kiddie junk—deflated wading pools, overturned wagons, Tonka trucks—most of it gnawed and chewed by the pudgy Bulldog (not a Mastiff) that came barking from beneath the trailer, following me at a distance to the door.

I knocked unsurely and waited for the sound

of footsteps from within, the rattling of a lock. Then the door opened and a woman with dark wet hair stuck her head out, giving me a cool once-over.

"Yeah?"

"Is...is Ray here?" I hesitated.

She blew an annoyed breath, the noise of a crying child floating from inside as she turned to walk away. I'd pulled my empty pack of Marlboros and went poking around inside—*yep, still empty*—when I heard the screaming, no longer a child's but the older, more experienced workings of an angry white woman: "*Shut up! Shuddup shuddup shuddup SHUDDUP! I don't CARE anymore—just get out! GET OUT!*"

Soon the screams gave way to tears, Dozer belting hellfire and steaming through the mud as the door veered back and this time it was Ray who stepped out, moving a little slower now as he saw me standing there with my no-shit expression. Great blue bags hung beneath his eyes and, though I'd missed it before, I noticed now that even his smile spoke of the scar, his secret always hidden somewhere behind those affable brown eyes like a burning itch that could never be scratched.

He moved down the steps, Dozer coming to lick gently at his fingers as Ray ran a hand over the dog's fat head.

"Let's take a walk," he said, motioning to nowhere. "Stay Dozer."

Dozer stopped, chomped a plastic shapeling from the yard, and settled lazily into his hole beneath the trailer. In no particular hurry, we picked our way to the road, my legs burning suddenly like two whips of fire as we strolled along the pavement.

"Last night wasn't the first time, you know," he said. "That I saw it? Your cousin's scar, I mean. The first time was two weeks ago, lying in bed down in Lafayette."

I nodded slowly, trying to understand. "I don't get it."

"I was down in Lafayette to buy a dredger from Stick Folsom. I'd been two days riding Greyhounds, seemed like two weeks. I hate talking on phones and I'd had plenty against my ear. I needed a break, needed to get away from it all, just for a little while. Of course, it was Sunday by then but I knew Prentice had done a show that weekend, I'd wanted to be here but Stick, he—" Ray stopped, coughed once, shook his head. "I couldn't make it. I couldn't be here and I needed a break so...I went back."

"Back?" I asked. "Back where?"

There was a moment of silence, but already I could hear the words, could taste them in the deep worries of my soul. And then he said it:

"I went back to the show, Wes. Back to Friday night."

"What do you mean you went *back*? The show was over."

"Just like I've went back to all the times and places I've went back to before. They all just kind of run together after a while, you know, like a bad dream. But not in all my years have I heard anything like what your cousin can do..."

"But Ray, that's..."

"That's *what? Impossible?*" Ray laughed then, a wild sort of look in his eyes. "I told you I wanted to experience everything this world has to offer—*everything*—if only once before I die. I told you I'd give anything, and I did. Just so happened that night I wanted to experience Prentice and so I climbed into bed and chose my place and chose my time...and I experienced.

"At first," he said, "I went and sat near Spike on the couch. Sat and listened to the music, listened to that incredible voice and just...*dreamed.* Dreamed of an existence that didn't so much resemble a living hell, of a life actually worth living one day at a time." Ray looked at me then, his eyes shining and full of secrets in the sun. "Time is a valuable thing, Wes. It never grows old. But one day it *will* end. Did you think it wouldn't?"

I said nothing, just stared at him. Legs quivering with every step as we kept down the road, and looking next the rounded pinnacle of the water tower had come breaching through the trees, eerie and foreboding.

"Finally I stood and moved up near the stage, staring out over the haze of teenage faces. But what I saw instead was an army. No different than Shiloh, really, no different than Gettysburg or Antietam, only this generation—they're pulling their own triggers. I watched your cousin, swept away, sweat dripping from every pore of his body until finally he slipped out of his shirt and...there it was. *The brand.*"

Ray laughed dolefully, not really meaning it.

"Hell, Wes, was like looking in a fuckin' mirror," he said. "I mean, I'd never seen anything like that on anyone else, never thought I would. Finally I couldn't take it anymore and got out, back up through the mist and out the other side and when I opened my eyes I was awake in Lafayette and my face was covered in tears. And for some reason, Wes...you were the first person I thought of."

Ray gave me a stare that was meant to be meaningful, leading me softly now down a twisted path through the trees. "And why me?" I asked. "What do I have to do with anyone else's mistakes? *Why are you telling me this?*"

"Not because it's what you want to hear," he told me. "But because I knew you'd care. 'Cause you're different, Wes, more different than even you'd like to admit, and I knew you'd go out of your way to help your cousin. Even when nobody else would."

"That's not true," I told him, believing it. "Prentice's mom would die for him if she could—and gladly do it. Besides, Prentice's death wish is his own business."

"Is it? 'Cause seems to me you two are the only family each other has left. Or haven't you noticed? You're the same: if Prentice dies, so do you."

An empty laugh. "And what would be so wrong with that?"

"Wes, you fear death just as much as you do life. If you didn't, you wouldn't be walking in these woods with me right now, stumbling like a drunk on a bender."

I had started to cry a little, and turned my face to wipe the tears.

"I knew you wouldn't believe me, of course," he told me. "And I don't blame you. I wouldn't believe a lot of the things I've seen—most of them, in fact. But I knew I needed *something*, something that could convince you, and so I went back again, this time to the first night we met. Do you remember that night? Friday, out in the Yard? The night you—"

His hand went for mine, and I swatted it away.

"And what can I do about that scar, Ray? Huh? How can I change it?"

"It's not too *late for him*, that's the difference. He isn't too far gone, not yet." He looked at me and said, "What if we could help him?"

I actually meant to laugh, but what came out instead was more like a groan. "Prentice doesn't want any help."

"Sure could use some, if you ask me. Don't fool yourself—Prentice *will* kill himself, Wes, one way or another."

He was right. I knew he was right, and hearing it said aloud suddenly I would do anything to change it. I'd seen the scar, after all, couldn't just turn back and pretend I hadn't. But was there any-thing I could do about it? Was there anything *anyone* could do? I wasn't so sure...

"*Can* it be changed?"

"Yes," Ray said. "I think it can, I absolutely do."

The trail broke then, opening on a beach and the soft crash of waves lapping endlessly at the shore. Stumbling closer, I stared over the water and couldn't help but feel somehow lost in this world, not really sure of my place at all. Only then the pain grew worse and, as I watched, a sudden fog rose like pale smoke across the beach, shrouding us against the sun. I reached out blindly, sensing for a moment Ray's rough hand on my shoulder before finally the fog turned dark, filling my vision, and before I could stop it my knees buckled and I felt myself falling...

THE
FIRE
INSIDE

I woke up on my porch.

It was night now, and looking over through the darkness I saw Ray hunched on the front steps; for a moment I stared, terrified in the moonlight at the prospect of his eyes glowing hellfire red, of scaly wings sprouting from his shoulders and pumping in the breeze. That would be all then, all for Weston Mercer, and next morning they'd find my remains scattered like so much fish chum over the porch.

Instead he stood, starting over—

"Stop. Don't come over here."

"The door was locked," he said, palms to the air. "I couldn't just leave you..."

"How did we get here?"

"I called a cab from Keri's. County Taxi, from Aurora. Same guy I got last night. He said he's getting to know these parts real good." Ray tried to laugh, swallowed hard instead, and looked to the road. "What's wrong with you, Wes?"

"Shut up, Ray."

"No—your legs? I mean, the way you just... gave out like that. Wes, that's not..."

"Not what? Not *normal?* Who are you to tell me anything about what's normal, Ray? No, you forfeited that right a long time ago..."

Silence.

Things were quiet for a while after that. That was a good thing, I needed that. Ray leaned against the post and must have counted cars as they passed, headed no doubt for Oyster Boulevard and then on to the Yard. And somewhere over the hum of crickets and power lines and of dogs barking at the moon, I could almost make out the sound of Olympus roaring down Prentice's mountain and washing over Reelsboro County, backed as always by the faint buzz of the Two Mad Gennies.

Yes, I could. It was faint but I could hear it just the same, the fast beat of Circean ritual ringing over the fields and calling down the faithful, the hardened hearts to dance. And for one endless moment I was convinced the music was sounding from somewhere deep inside of *me*, welling up in deep waves over my heart.

I stood carefully, staggering to the end of the porch and spitting over the rail.

"I was sixteen too, Ray," I said, wiping my mouth. "Only I wasn't running away from home or looking for Haight-Ashbury or drinking electric Kool-Aid, I was just..."

"Wes..."

"*I was minding my own fucking business!*"

As if reading my mind, Ray pulled a pack of menthols from his faded leather jacket—Keri's, he told me—and tossed it over. I tapped out a cigarette and put it to work.

"I had my first job that summer," I told him. "Me and Dan both, working the grain bins for Blackwell's dad. Some nights we'd stay late on the farm—we'd have supper, or hang back and bullshit and grease the machines. Then driving home one night there was this big storm through Lancer County—and Lancer, once you get out that far, ain't much left but cows and combines anyway."

Ray laughed weakly, moonlight bringing out the web of crow's feet around his eyes and, for the first time, the tell-tale signs of ringworm on his face.

"With all the rain, I didn't notice the headlights till the last second..."

I took in a drag, nice and long, blew it out. *Ah, sweet song of emphysema...*

"Had on my seat belt but what really held me in was the truck itself—crunched on me like a cheap can of sardines." I glanced down, patting at each of my knees. "On these."

I closed my eyes, and suddenly that night—the

headlights, the screeching tires, and everything after, after, after—it all took on an unnaturally detached clarity, a lucidity that could now, finally, be interpreted through the years.

"They had to cut me open to save my life—*ccchhh!*—right down the middle." I pulled a finger down the center of my chest. "Gutted, just like a deer."

Hoots and catcalls from over the hills, a smattering of applause.

I looked him in the eyes and said, "I died that night, you know. Literally."

Ray only stared, his face alive with a dreadful sort of wonder.

"What was it like?"

I thought about it, dragging my smoke and tossing it away.

"I couldn't tell you, Ray. I wasn't there."

Now the tears again, a hot slap across my face and this time there was no hiding them as I glanced to Ray and the sudden finality behind those dark brown eyes. I sobbed and shook and it all really did make me want to puke, but I lit another cigarette instead. I was mourning the loss of myself.

I told him about the surgeries, a series of nightmare operations meant to put me back together but that seemed only to draw out the pain. About sleeping in a morphine haze and the feeling of being a ghost as people hovered around and spoke in murmured tones about your "condition."

"When something like that happens in a

small town," I told him, "there's a lot of gossip goes around. Lots of visitors, lots of cards, pretty flowers. Hell, you woulda thought I *had* died out there—for good, I mean—and actually that *was* part of the story, at one point. But when everybody had done their good little deed and made a call or put their card in the mail, what was left? Me. Rolling around in a wheelchair for eleven months, hobbling on crutches after that..."

The music had stopped now—Intermission, I knew, the middle of the set—and in the sudden silence that followed I lifted my shirt, watching the cold expression on Ray's face as he studied the scar down the middle of my chest. His eyes dipped furtively against the moon, and I imagined a tear at the corner of one eye.

I dropped my shirt and turned away.

"The other driver, turns out she was smashed on moonshine and so we all lawyered up and settled out of court. She, uh...at the settlement hearing, she showed up with her arm in one of those slings and this ridiculous pillow strapped around her neck. Then I rolled in and I think I made the whole bunch of 'em blush. Two weeks later I had twenty grand waiting for me on the other side of eighteen. That's down to two, and I'll probably have arthritis by the time I'm thirty."

Ray was silent a moment, then shrugged.

"Well, at least you'll always know when a storm's coming."

We both smiled, morbid, genuine smiles. For

a while, things were quiet; the night settling into a lull of howls and the distant sounds of motors revving high, the wind sweeping in eddies through the yard. Ray walked over, dropping a hand on my shoulder.

"Wes, I'm sorry..."

"Don't mention it."

"But if there's any kind of providence in opportunity—and I believe there is—I may just be able to lend you a hand with your money troubles..."

I looked at him then, and saw that his face had taken on a strange, weary-eyed expression. He shuffled back to the steps, and for the first time I noticed the shadow of a wide duffel bag at his feet. He poked at it lightly with the tip of his boot.

"You wouldn't happen to have a spare room would you?"

§

Keri had kicked him out, of course. No surprises there.

She stopped by the next morning and she and Ray headed back to Fairfield to pack up his things. While they were gone, I put on some Motown and found some charcoal and tried to sketch a little something, an old habit that had sometimes served as a kind of therapy for me, a meditation.

But that kinda therapy just wasn't possible today; it was too hot for that kind of thing. So I stripped down to undies and watched some Classic TV. A *Lucy*, some *Happy Days*. It was a Saturday afternoon and I had nothing better to do than watch Potsie sing "Pumps Your Blood" for the umpty-umpth time, or the episode where Joanie goes greaser and gets caught up in that mess in the school gym. "*You put out an advertisement,*" the Fonz had said, "*and somebody's gonna answer that ad.*"

Only then *The Munsters* was coming on and after the theme song I tuned out. So instead of *Gilligan's Island*, I found myself watching scrambled porn on Channel 98. Which was basically the same thing. Funny thing was, even as I lay there poking around in my tightie-whities and coming to the slow realization my life had become something out of Stephen King, I really wasn't studdin' the TV at all—what I really wanted was to *stop thinking so much*.

But it was impossible. My mind was restless, always running in some weird direction I didn't want it going, and I would've just about killed to slow things down a little. People call that sort of thing "panic attack" or "breakdown," but to me it seemed more like *Night of the Living Dead*—HOME EDITION: I'd hear a creak from the kitchen and there was Prentice, tongue old and dry as it spat like putty from his mouth; the rustling of leaves on the porch, and this time it was Ray, skin mouldered as he whispered darkly about how time will kill us all. Even Aunt Joyce made an appearance, eyes crazed, Bible gripped in one trembling hand as she began literally beating me over the head. "*You've ruined your life!*" she'd scream. "*Ruined it, ya little smut-hound! Now burn!* **BURN. BUUUUUR- RRRNNNN!'**

There was one thing I didn't have to worry about for the time being, and that was cash. In return for letting him crash till things got straightened out with Keri—or until the ink had dried on his deal with Stick Folsom—Ray had offered to put me in clover. Which was fine by me. Great flaming reams of sheep dip, with that type of talk Ray could squat as long as his little heart desired... or at least until my landlord Morty got wise and kicked him out—hell, probably kicked us *both* out.

But I didn't care. Beggars can't be choosers, and the day a man becomes poor is the day he's used his last favor in the world's eyes. At last money was not a concern, at least temporarily; I was, however, becoming increasingly obsessed with death.

Later that afternoon, Ray and Keri returned and I helped them load his stuff onto the porch: seven or eight cardboard boxes, a few garbage bags of clothes and shoes, a complete collection of useless eight-tracks. Then I went back inside and gave them a chance to talk, maybe work out some of their kinks, despite the feeling these were some pretty serious kinks. Finally, I heard the dull buzz of the Jeep pulling away (Keri's shift started at four, Ray told me, and sometimes Keith let her in early to put down table cloths or sweep at the floors), and stepping onto the porch I found Ray sitting there in much the same position as the night before, only now instead of one stuffed gym bag he was surrounded by a dizzying mix of liquor boxes, each filled with something he no longer had a place for. Useless junk.

I asked him, "What now?"

Ray said nothing, however, only limped pitifully on the steps, head pressed down dramatically into his hands. I heard a low whimpering and, after a moment, noticed the slow jump of his shoulders, the subtle trembling up his spine, then turned quietly and went back inside.

§

That night we had the bonfire.

We'd collected a few hunks of firewood and spent a good hour or so raking the pine straw into piles in the backyard, and then, after lugging Ray's boxes from the porch, found two cinder blocks and moved those out to the site. Ray had grabbed a sixer on his way back from Fairfield, as well as a handful of cigars—those went out to the site. And as night fell over Reelsboro County and vehicles roared past on their way to the Yard, we'd gathered together and cracked respective beers, and then slowly set about tossing the remains of Ray's long years into the flames.

I hadn't put much thought into those boxes, into what types of things they might hold or just why Ray would want to burn whatever it was instead of, say, hauling it to Big Oke's landfill like a normal person. But it didn't take long to realize these were not your usual pack-rat items.

I opened the first box of vanished Wild Irish

Rose, and there was a Popeye mug brimming with gold doubloons; beneath that, a withered form of Philistine pottery. The next—a faded box of tequila—held Polaroid photographs of a Ray Lafargue only slightly younger than the one who sat before me now, his diminutive form posing with a Stratocastered Jimi Hendrix, a Beatles-era Lennon and McCartney, Teddy Roosevelt on horseback at the Panama Canal. The next batch was a shaky bunch of pictures featuring dead soldiers on the banks of Normandy and Cemetery Ridge, of the Tunguska fireball and the Calcutta cyclone. Up next was a series of shots taken from the tops of Everest and Angel Falls. The red crab migration on Christmas Island. Snaps of Alhambra and Machu Picchu. The Pyramids of Giza. The great Northern Lights.

I looked, and the stack of Polaroids piled to the bottom of the box.

Ray had opened a similar box of photos and sat tossing them by handfuls into the fire. I rushed at him now, toppling my beer as I grabbed the pictures from his hands—*snatched* them from his hands, really.

"Whatdya think you're doin', huh!"

Ray appeared confused. "I'm getting rid of all this...this *stuff*, Wes. None of this matters anymore."

"Of course it matters, this is—this is unbelievable! We can't just..."

It's not that I hadn't believed Ray before—I *had*, even when I wished I didn't—but this, these things, made it real in a whole new way. My eyes had been opened, and now I surveyed the worn boxes—some strayed along the grass, many already too close to the fire—as if seeing them for the first time.

For a moment, I was speechless.

"You bastard, why didn't you show me these before?"

But already Ray was staring at another of the pictures; the photo showed what appeared to be a startled Cistercian monk. He flipped to the next, and there were waves of people bowed adoringly beneath the spires of a golden temple. Another flip, and what could have only been the conquest of Mecca, with perhaps Muhammad himself staring back with wild sage eyes.

"I stopped that business with the camera a long time ago. Some things are only meant for here," he said, tapping two well-bitten fingers to his temple. For a moment he looked like one of those people who can bend silverware with their minds. "And as for this stuff, these pictures...they're okay, but they fold under the persuasion of denial. Denial is a powerful thing, Wes, and to fight it—to *really* fight it—you need to hit 'em where it hurts. Or else all this"—a sweep of the boxes—"doesn't amount to much more than a basement full of doctored photographs and stage props."

Stage props or not, a part of me wanted to grab these boxes and hurry them inside, where I would spend the next several years going over and over them, and me and Prentice and Spike asking Ray all sorts of dumb questions about what he'd seen and where this shot was taken and what made him want to go and see thing like that. Yes, we would have all-night storytimes where—

But then I saw the look in Ray's face, and stopped.

They weren't my memories.

I realized that suddenly: *they weren't my memories* and I had no right to take them from him.

And besides, I thought, what could I really gain from a photo album of Ray Lafargue and his golden oldie moments? Hadn't I been living vicariously for long enough? Long enough without Ray being added to the mix?

So instead I took a seat, grabbed my near-empty bottle from the ground, and helped him throw all the photos, the etched totems and terra cotta figures, the small autograph collection—bearing names like Napoleon Bonaparte, Benjamin Franklin, Beethoven—into the fire. As we worked, the faint buzz of the Gennies could be heard from on high (the sound had been heralded by a row of feel-good applause) and now the music was cranked and raining down like snowfall through the trees. Yes, the Saturday Night Revival was in full swing—and yet, for the second time that week, it was a show I had no desire to attend.

"Besides, it was all a trick," Ray said finally, as the music rolled. "All I wanted was to *experience*, to see the world just once for all it's worth...but I can't even do that." He threw an empty box into the fire.

"But all the stories you've told me...all this..."

I gestured to the boxes of old photographs, souvenirs, artifacts. With something like horror, I noticed half of them had already been emptied into the fire.

"Do you know how long the world has been around, Wes? 'Cause I sure don't. And all this"—another sweep of the boxes—"all this is less than fifteen hundred years' worth of junk. A drop in the bucket, Wes—that's all they gave me, as far back as I'm allowed. That's what I sold myself for. *Fifteen hundred years,*" he said the words again, only this time they came out with bite, a weak sarcasm.

"Why fifteen hundred?" I asked, not understanding. "Why not two hundred or four hundred—why not four *thousand?* I mean, what if you could—"

Ray cut me off with his hand.

"I've tried. Oh, I've tried until I couldn't move. But the *burning.*"

"What burning?"

"Call it a *boundary,*" he told me. "Something that happens when you hit the outer limits, when you reach too far back. I'd felt it first on a trip to the Dark Ages, got my first blisters following the great Antioch quake of 526. At the time I thought it was nothing, a nuisance more than anything. I could put up with a few nasty blisters, sure, no problem. What's a little rug burn?"

I snickered, and tossed in a priceless coil of

pearls.

"And so one night I decided to push the limits, and set out on the longest journey of all. I'd settled down, climbed into bed like I'd done a thousand times before, and fixed my spirit where I wanted to go: Pompeii, Italy, A.D. 74."

My mind flashed back to sixth grade, to Mrs. Bell's history class and the memory of figures turned to stone, of an entire city transformed into ash and frozen in time.

My eyes narrowed: "*Vesuvius*. The volcano."

Ray nodded. "The mist came up, like it always does. The long dark tunnel, the vibrations, the pull. I wasn't halfway in when..." He paused, eyes dancing with memory; I didn't know what was in there, didn't want to find out. "I climbed out fast as I could, but the damage had been done. Blisters the size of walnuts had come up both legs—both legs, and more besides—and my chest was burning so bad it felt like somebody had my heart on a spit. Hell, I'd even pissed the sheets." He smiled miserably. "In other words, it was the worst sunburn of my life."

A soft wind blew past, brushing through the trees. In the distance, Olympus continued to writhe and thrust.

"I don't understand..."

"*Limits*," Ray said. "Consider it the small print, same as with any contract. Apparently, the other side has kept up the tradition. I've come to terms with my decision since then—if that's possible—

but I'll never forgive myself for it." His eyes locked with mine over the fire. "And neither will your cousin."

I leaned forward, finally asking the question that had bothered me ever since our walk down the Marsten Road. The one thing that'd been on my mind more than anything else...but it was also the thing that scared me most. Now the words came simply and without fear.

"You said we could help him. How?"

For a moment Ray was silent, staring into the flames.

"Wes, I wanted to see it all, to run the gamut of human experience," he said. "That was my passion. I don't know what your cousin's passion is—why he did what he did, or what he did it for. But it doesn't matter. It's done. And if he's going through anything like what I did those first few years, he's scared. He's alone. Sometimes he's as scared of it as you are...but he also craves it. Right now, he's maybe not so sure what to make of it, but what he doesn't realize is that eventually it won't matter, because it will rule him. If he lets it—and we both know he will—*it will rule him*. You've already seen some of that, I know."

He shook his head, lifting another nothing and tossing it into the fire, the flames pushing higher, higher. In the light, I noticed Ray's beard had now grown into a complete shade over the bottom half of his face.

"Prentice has lost himself," he said. "He's

broken; something inside is missing and he needs healing. That's what it all comes to, Wes—he needs *healing*. And to get that he needs a healer, someone who can find that missing piece and bring it back. Do you understand?"

I did. I'd witnessed that look in Prentice's eyes, after all, just before the blackness had taken over completely: an evil mirror that cast some darker resemblance of my cousin to the world. But then I couldn't help but feel I'd lost a bit of myself, as well, that maybe *I* could use some healing too, dammit.

"Fine, but how do we *do* that?"

Ray gulped his beer. "You remember the night we first met? Down in the Yard? The night you—"

"I *remember*, Ray." I kept waiting for him to reach over and grab my hand, maybe talk all night about how that old banana-seat bike just flew and flew before smacking that pine, yes sir, you really pitched that one, Wes, you really—

"Well, do you remember Taco? Mexican guy?"

"Sure, the grass man. Gives bad deals to Vanceboro kids who don't know what a bad deal is."

"That's the one."

"What about him?"

"We used to boat together a few years back, before his legs got too bad for it. Scalloped mostly, outta Newport News. But one night...well, one night something happened to us out there. Something I'd never seen before..."

I looked and Ray had pulled out another of

his cigars, was leaned forward and lighting it at the edge of the fire. He puffed away and said: "Back in those days a couple guys made extra dough hauling dope on the water. You know, connecting the dots. It wasn't so dangerous to do things like that back then, and a lot of folks even made it rich because of it. Duke Spain was into that sort of thing—him and Jim Cole, Big Nelson Struthers, couple other guys—and anyway that's what we were doing on that trip. It didn't take long for them to start dipping into the supply, and sure enough, things got out of control. Mark Halpern was swinging from the outrigger, Duke passed out on top of the wheelhouse. Couple women so high they'd almost drowned themselves skinny-dipping."

But it's what happened afterwards, he said, that changed him forever.

How long afterwards he wasn't sure, only that he'd woken in the night to find everyone passed out and Taco collapsed on the deck, both hands clutching at his chest. He was shaking and calling out, gurgling for words, his face turned strangely pale against the moon. Ray had staggered to his feet, and was moving toward him through the darkness when he turned and...

"And that's when I saw him," he said simply. "Stumbling over in a slow sleepwalker stagger, only there was something *else*, something...it's like he wasn't even *human* anymore. Taco was barely conscious but he saw it too, kicking up his legs while the guy walked over and put two hands down over his chest. Then—**BOOM**—like a gun going off, and all these colors up around Taco and that man. And Wes, one of 'em went straight into *Taco's chest*."

I swallowed hard, so hard it hurt. "What was it?"

"I don't know," he said. "I suppose I'll never know. Taco told me later it felt like some big tooth being pulled out of his chest. Whatever it was took away his heart problem like that"—*snap!*—"and I also believe it saved his life." Ray puffed at his cigar, running a hand through his curly dark hair. "Next morning we sat around a good three hours trying to figure if we'd actually saw what we *thought* we'd seen, if the whole thing had really happened at all. We decided it had. We remembered it the same, after all—but we were the only ones. The other fella, Mr. Fists of Fire? Didn't remember a thing. Not past the coke and the booze and whatever else he'd been jumpin' on the night before. Not a *thing*."

"Did you tell him what happened?"

Ray laughed. "Would you? No, me and Taco talked about it but in the end neither of us could bring ourselves to do it. And besides, he wasn't there anyway."

I made a face. "What do mean he *wasn't there?*"

"It wasn't him, don't you get it? It wasn't him doing anything—it's like something was working *through* him. I can't tell you what it was, but *something* came over that guy. Then it all started to click when we got back and I did a little digging, found out where he was actually from. That his family wasn't local at all, had only moved here from out west when he was born."

"Big whoop."

"But wait, it gets better. 'Cause when you dig back a few generations you start to see something. You start to see that this is no ordinary family, that they're more like something out of Castaneda. Healers, yes, but after their own peculiar breed, with their own ceremonies and artifacts. *Shamans*, Wes. Have you heard of them?"

I had. Ritual healers, medicine men, psycho-babblers. *Witch doctors*, I thought.

"He doesn't have much to do with his parents anymore—hates them, in fact. But, like it or not, I guess some things just run in the family..."

Another gust of wind, and a chill slowly laid its hands over my spine.

"I lied to you about one thing," he said. "I told you when I came back that night in Lafayette that you were the first person I thought of. And you were close—you were second—but this guy... he was the first. But it's you, Wes, *you* were what made the difference this time. So, to answer your question: yes, there is someone who can help your cousin. And he stays right here in Carolina."

Ray took a long swig from his beer. It was perhaps the longest swig I'd ever seen Ray Lafargue take, of anything.

"You told me Prentice sleeps after every Saturday night show?" he asked. "That you could set a watch by it?"

"Always," I said, and couldn't help but think of all the drugs that go coursing through my cousin's body in a week's time, of his poor little liver and sad, struggling heart. *He sleeps*, I thought, *but only because he has to, only because his body makes him.* And without thinking: "He crashes."

"He should be unconscious then, which is good—and alone, which is best. I told you this guy stays nearby. Well, if we can get him up there—which should be a lot easier than you might think—then maybe your cousin can get the healing he needs."

"But that was a *heart attack*, Ray. I mean, that was *physical* and this is—"

"No, actually it's not that different. Sickness is a relative thing, and whatever was working through this guy that night, it healed what was there—it healed whatever was laid on its plate—and I'm convinced it will do the same the next time. Physical, mental, whatever. If there's anybody in this world who can help your cousin, I believe this person can."

Something occurred to me then. "If you're so sure, then why hasn't this guy helped you? Why haven't you—"

"What happened on the water that night was a once-in-a-lifetime event, I'm not denying that. And if you think I haven't thought about what you're asking at least a thousand times, you're wrong. But the truth is..." He paused, casting another of his lonesome gazes into the fire. "Truth is I'm not worth it, Wes. Your cousin is. My life is over—I've made my little bed, and that's fine—but Prentice's is just beginning."

We were quiet a moment, Ray tossing photos and meaningless knick-knacks into the fire, me watching him, wanting to comfort him, to say something that didn't seem so morbidly fatalistic, but it wouldn't come. Finally, Ray broke the silence:

"There's one thing."

Then dread, like a lump in the pit of my stomach. "What one thing?"

"I told you he didn't remember a thing. That for all intents and purposes this guy wasn't there. He wasn't there, and he shouldn't be there this time either. Somewhere between the sleeplessness and the dope—he'd went down, stepped out." Ray said this simply, matter-of-fact, the way one might speak of losing a spare set of keys. "He'd worked himself into a trance—most of those guys had—and we believe that's the only reason what happened that night *did* happen. But the difference is this guy has the *power*, he has the *gift*—his whole family does. But the only way this will work—the only way he'll let it come out, you see—is if he's in the same state of mind he was in that night."

Fantastic, I thought. *We'll just walk over to the guy's house, hold a gun to his head, force him to his feet for oh eighteen hours—no catnaps for good behavior—then jam about three shelves of Bynum Pharmacy down his throat. No problem. Sure thing Ray, old buddy, I'm sure he'll coop-*

erate right up until the second he drops dead...

Ray pulled something from his jeans pocket, looked at it, held it out.

I took and rolled it in my palm, examining it. It looked, I thought, like a rock—a dark stone polished to smooth perfection. I leaned into the light to get a better look.

"What is it?"

"It's not what all those guys had been putting into their bodies that night," he told me, "but it is a lot better. And whatever it was on that boat, whatever was working through him that night...this should bring it out."

I glanced over at him, then back to the small reflective stone. I didn't get it.

Finally, Ray said, "We'll put it in his drink. He won't know a thing."

"In his *drink?*"

"That's the way it's been done for centuries."

"What is it?"

"It'll work."

"Well...where'd you *get* it?" It felt soft, warm.

"I procured it on one of my many trips. It came from long ago, and had existed for a long time before I found it. Much imitated but never duplicated, more potent than the vapors that inspired the Pythia, the Delphic Oracle. Bowls of them graced the tables of Jannes and Jambres before Pharaoh. This'll make getting high seem like a nice bowel movement."

"But Ray, what if—"

"It won't hurt him, he'll be just fine. He'll sleep for about twelve hours, he'll wake up, and he won't know a thing except he feels like a million bucks and it must've been a great show. Won't remember a thing."

Something in the way he said that made me look at him. He was peering down at a picture, and for only a moment a thin sadness washed over his face. Then I asked the question I'd been waiting to be answered all along:

"Who is it?"

Ray stared at me, the mystery still swirling deep in his eyes as the first flashes of blue light splashed across the yard. It was still dancing over the trees when I turned and noticed the police cruiser braking to a slow stop near the house. Moments later the lights faded, leaving only the softly flickering flames of the fire as—

The fire.

But it was too late.

Already the figure was upon us, strolling across the grass and over to the fire and, stepping into the light, I recognized him right off—Mike Lunsmann, small-town Deputy Dawg and budding Olympus enthusiast.

"Quite a fire," he said, and all of a sudden I wasn't so sure I was getting out of this. Lunsmann was the one who'd almost given me that citation the year before.

"Well," I laughed, "it runs on wood and straw, officer—no more, no less." This I said even as three of the near-empty liquor boxes sat around the fire—and the charred remains of two still *inside*. The idea of Mike getting too close to those boxes suddenly made me uneasy, and I'd started to my feet when—

"Don't stand," Mike said. "Just stay right there."

So I stayed. That's when I looked and saw Ray was no longer beside me; also gone was that peculiar slick stone out of my hand. From the corner of my eye I caught something moving through the trees and realized it was the cherry of Ray's cigar; I didn't know it at the time, but he was saving me a lot of trouble down the road by not being seen with me that night.

I watched as Mike circled the fire several times, pretending to eye it closely though I'm sure he had a fairly accurate read of the situation. He peered briefly into one of the boxes—action figures, mostly, couple books by Dr. Seuss—and then gazed toward the house, sniffing as he eyed the mounting pile of garbage near the back door. He bent low, gracefully plucking a Budweiser from the ground, then popped the top and inhaled half.

"Well," he said, wiping his mouth, "I can see you're just burning a little pine straw here. I know, me and the old lady do the same thing. Just seems to pile up on you sometimes."

"—it *does*—"

"You just be sure and keep it *contained*. Containment is the issue. Trust a fire only as far as you can throw it, understand?"

"Yes, sir."

Mike finished the beer with a quick gulp. "Sort of figured you'd be up to your cousin's by now..."

I told him yeah, that I'd gotten a late start and was just getting ready to leave—as soon as I put out the fire, of course.

"Mm. Long walk. Need a ride?"

I pretended to think. "Nah, Mike, you go on. I'll be fine." *You think that's a long walk, you're crazy. You should try the mountain sometime, tubby.* "Here, take one for the road."

I held out a beer.

Mike eased it from my hand, and glancing briefly I could make out the remains of some pretty decent muttonchops running the sides of his face. In the distance, small music rolled over the hills.

"Suit yourself," he said. "But I tell you, I sure wouldn't want whatever got ahold of that James Harrell fella gettin' ahold of you..."

I didn't say anything, and for a long time neither did Mike.

"Harrell seems to think it was a...some type of *animal*," he told me. "Bobcat maybe—too dark to tell, he says. But there's been talk about finding it, whatever it was...and killing it."

A fuzzy scene direct from *Lord of the Flies* flashed before my eyes. I wanted to laugh, but with growing horror found I couldn't so much as breathe. What was he...was he *threatening* me now? Threatening *us?* Was that what he was doing? I mean, why would Mike go and say a stupid thing like that for anyway? *Screw him. Truly, in his ear with a western steer...*

"Now you be sure and put this fire out good, Weston. And watch it, don't get these boxes too close. They're sure to catch. These woods so close on you here, a brush fire is the last thing this county needs. Especially on a friggin' *Saturday night.*"

Mike stared into the trees. After a moment, he hitched his pants and spat a little something into the grass, then passed the fire for a final time, his big black belt shining like waxed leather in the night. At last I could make out the small squeak of his shoes as they carried him across the yard.

"You take it easy, Wes," he called. "And remember what I said about them boxes. I'd hate to come back, see they'd gotten to close after all..."

I told him sure thing, Mike, will do, then flashed a tall middle finger at the back of his head, and with that he was gone. I heard the slam of his car door, the low rumble of the cruiser cranking up. The strobes resumed, momentarily lighting the trees, and were immediately silenced. Then he was off, my wearied eyes watching as he sped down Kershaw and off toward the Yard and another serving of free booze and kiss-ass.

It was a long time before Ray came out of the woods.

Puddles dotted the sidewalk along Oyster Boulevard—scattered remnants of the hard rain the night before—and despite the sun burning bright and low on the horizon, I couldn't help but feel a kind of chill hanging in the air. Apparently Ray felt it, too: both hands stuffed in his faded leather jacket, a deep thicket of beard highlighted by fateful sprigs of gray causing a sort of half-mask to fall over his face. A large ringworm festered beneath one eye.

For two weeks we'd been turning things over and over in our heads, consulting vague theories on order and accountability, and the undying bonds of family and the question of ends justifying means, combing them over with military-like precision.

There were no stones left unturned; we had everything in place and everything that wasn't in place, we were putting there.

We'd gotten word Spike was back in town—returned again from his voyage at sea—something confirmed earlier that afternoon as Ray and I hiked out to the old Budget Inn; the manager told us Spike had checked in late the night before, then muttered something only slightly resembling a room number and was forever silenced by the end of a commercial run. He was watching *Dallas*.

And while there was no answer at Room 134, several of Spike's bags still lay empty on the tumbledown bench outside. We left a note on the door: ERN'S 8 PM.

I'd talked to Prentice only once since that fateful trip to the Herring House, the two of us bumping into each other one morning as I went around trafficking garbage to the local bins. Among other things, he informed me he'd pulled the plug on Olympus's Saturday night shows, at least for the time being—"until I get a little more respect from these non-honoring blowhards."

Respect.

That's what he'd called it. But I think it wasn't that at all. Sure, maybe those schwag offerings *had* gotten a little old—especially as winter closed in— but I think the real reason Prentice put an end to those Saturday shows was that *he just couldn't handle the extra night.* I think the dope had become too much for him—that yes, he'd fallen in love with a trained killer—and his system just couldn't take it anymore, couldn't take the abuse, the addiction, and had started crashing early on him. No surprises there; I knew the drill. Only now instead of sleeping Sundays and waking late Monday afternoon, well, now he'd snooze straight through the weekend and rise early Monday morning, ready for another five days of death on tap and anything goes and gimme what ya got.

He was running late that morning, and walking away he told me I'd better come up sometime, better get up with him, be there this Friday. But they were words spoken out of necessity, and had it been anyone else—anyone besides good cousin Wes—they wouldn't have been said at all. Sad thing was, we both kind of knew it, too.

He looked horrible, his hair grown disgustingly dry and having lost that full, buoyant wave that had always happened so naturally. His skin appeared milky, almost contagious, his frame little more than a rock-school scarecrow; even his clothes seemed thinner, and carried with them a peculiar, acrid stench.

We hadn't spoken since.

The following Friday night, after a long afternoon of sleep, Ray and I listened with mounting anxiety, waiting, wondering if there would be a show at all. There had been. It had started later than usual, but there *had* been one. And though we couldn't bring ourselves to visit the Yard and join the circus proper—not now, not yet—we'd waited until the music faded and then set out across town, down Oyster Boulevard and Hall's Creek Road and finally up the mountain itself. As the morning sun rose high over a distant horizon, at last we'd breached the barn and—just as I knew we would—found his silent body stowed away beyond the amps, past the stage in that small room to the back. His face shone pale in the darkness...

Next week, Ray had said, gazing with wonder at his silent ghoulish form. *Next week...*

Now Ernul's appeared up ahead, rising in a mirage against the smoky skyline, and without thinking I began to finger the quarter hanging on a string around my neck. Stepping inside, Ray spun a wearied glance over the bar and all at once everyone was twisting in their stools, their faces a chorus of aw-shucks nods and grins; others back-slapped us with pride. Bill Fowler, who managed his own farm supply store here in town, bought me a beer and gave me an evil *I now own your soul* smirk.

Again, nothing had really changed. Thursdays were still better than Fridays, more intimate in our suffering and without all the riffraff, and walking into the bar that night was like walking into a scene in a movie you've watched a thousand times. Most of these knuckleheads I could list down the backside of one leg, and what they drank down the other.

I checked Ray's watch. Seven-thirty. Good.

We pushed back through the crowd and settled at our booth, where despite knowing every nuance of its existence—every scribbled oath and foul invective, every scattered chip and stain—the table was now as foreign to me as anything I'd ever known. It struck me I couldn't fathom a time when life had made less sense, and with it a nagging sensation that at any moment I might collapse to my knees in tears, overcome by the sadness of being alive.

Three beers later I was laughing right out loud because Moe, Larry, and Curly were acting up for these three butt-ugly women that really were atrocious and who looked strangely like the Stooges themselves. Along with the sound effects, this was hilarious. I noticed that Moe was always bossing everybody around—bonking them, tweaking their noses, cracking skulls—which sort of bothered me. He'd always acted that way, always king shit. I wondered why, and decided it was probably because he could sock harder than any one of 'em. Curly had the weight advantage, sure, and if he applied himself I think he could've positively obliterated somebody's face; but little old Moe, he had the *fury*. If somebody did something stupid, he was the one who wouldn't hesitate to slug them over the head with a pipe or ball-peen hammer.

Now Shemp, Shemp could've been a contender if he hadn't been so docile, so flaccid. His flaccidity blew it for him as head Stooge. Ray nudged me with the end of his bottle, and my head followed his directions in operating a turn.

And there, standing in the open door across

the bar—was Spike.

He stepped inside, a whisper of emerald-colored leaves swirling in at his feet. His eyes, large and goofy behind the thick magnifiers of his glasses, moved from stool to booth and back again, enlightening him once more with the way things were, had been, and threatened to always be. And muttering somewhere beneath the clattering glasses and groans of uninspired laughter, an agile festering assured him that he, too, was part of the moving death. *Sit down*, it said, *have a drink. You too are part of the slippery black death. Have a cold one. Might as well be on me.*

Spike hesitated, then caught a glimpse of my raised hand at the back of the bar.

He'd started toward us when I realized the bastard was actually wearing some fresh clothes: the blue jeans were still blue, but brand-new Levi's as dark as a thousand midnights reflected off the sea; his faded flannel exchanged for an unbearably red cashmere jacket, the gut-grabber beneath for a Hanes as white as anything in the bar.

He lunged forward, arms collapsing around me in a tight bear hug that sent his glasses leaping across the table. Ray reached to hand them over, Spike turning suddenly and taking a firm two-fingered grip on his beard.

"Grizzly Adams, I presume?" he said, laughing, until then he caught sight of the nickel-sized growth beneath Ray's eye and the laughter died. Spike's own beard, once a confusing maze of crumbs and dead insects, had retreated to a shade along the contours of his face.

"Look at this, Ray," I said. "Spike went and got all dolled up for us, ain't that sweet?"

"He's never looked so dreamy," Ray added.

"Oh, he's gorgeous. He really is."

But Spike only grinned and cracked his beer, watching as the ghosts circuited the bar and spun smoke signals at the moon, slowly biding their time.

Things are good, that reasonable, rational voice spoke up. *Things are good and there's no need to go forming any half-cocked theories, no need to get cold feet. Hasn't there been enough of that already? A wise person once told me: time stops for no man. No man, not even death himself.* I looked, and now Moe was in the middle of a courtroom, attempting to coax some colorless talking bird from its small colorless cage. He was saying: *here polly polly polly, here polly polly. Here polly polly polly polly. Here polly.*

"Looks like much hasn't changed around here," Spike said, brown eyes rolling slowly over the stools. "Small crowd, must be a Thursday. Winos unite. Babysitters are holding out for tomorrow, double rates after twelve. Wait, I do see a few empty stools—Buddy Respers comes to mind, so does Petey Havlicek. Who else? Anybody died I need to know about?"

"Nobody died," Ray gushed, "just smells like they did, that's all."

More laughter, only this time others seemed to join in, slapping at knees and their toothless grins turned to the sky. These were the same people who conducted group sing-alongs of "Joy to the World" and "The Ballad of Curtis Loew," and pretty much any song by Charlie Daniels. Film of choice: *Smokey and the Bandit.* Average number of years left to live: twenty-three-point-eight.

Ray asked about his trip, and Spike went on to describe ideal weather conditions on the water, near-perfect sunsets, sunrises backed by gulls. Nights when the sky was so clear, he said, that stars turned the sea into something like one long sheet of ice. Gone was the creeping stress and suicidal tendencies which seemed to follow him during stints with the Dave Chabons and Kevin Hillebrandts of the world; back as never before was that misunderstood wisdom and goofy good humor that had first drawn me to Spike all those years ago.

He was still going on about all this when he stopped suddenly, the smile fading from his face.

"Uh oh," he said. "Here we go..."

It was Prentice, his black-clad figure spewed through the front door like a vomit from some dark, cavernous throat. Already people were spinning in their seats, some stumbling over to him with crumpled bills or baggies; others muttered quietly, faces narrowed on his ghostly frame.

He nodded madly as he spoke, eyes wide and deranged and blotted with pupil; smoke gathered in small, eerie clouds at his shoulders. No sooner had it collected than the mob dispersed and Prentice strode smoothly away, shadowed by a curly-haired boy I'd never seen before.

He came over and patted our shoulders, gave us smiles and little nods. Ran a few fingers over Spike's bright cashmere jacket and told him he looked red as a communist, what the hell was he thinking?

"Look who's talking," Spike said. "Think you need a shower, bud, soon as you get done robbing that bank...or sacrificing those kittens, whichever you finish last."

The boy with curls stepped forward.

"Fellas, this here's Skeeter," Prentice said. "Gonna be drumming with us for a while, just filling in, you know. As you may have heard, Rick, uh...well, Rick has contracted tuberculosis. Terrible tragedy, I know, but we're moving past it..."

Skeet's head bounced as Prentice spoke, and watching them I was reminded again of the last time we'd been gathered together here. Of how bad Prentice looked as he wandered into the bar that night, black-clad in crumbling leather, and how much worse he looked now. Ray, meanwhile, had grown a three-story beard, and Spike had cashed out for a new wardrobe.

Maybe some things had changed after all.

Prentice collapsed into the booth, the four of us crowding to make room for Skeeter and settling into our normal routine of cigarettes and booze, conversations whirling round and round till nobody knew where they started or where they might end, or maybe if they wouldn't.

"Ya'll gotta see m'bike," Prentice would say. "Had some good times, me and m'bike. Even wiped out t'other day—remember that Skeet? When I wiped out? The **ROOT?**" He tilted the sleeve of his duster, his pitiful finger dangling there like a dirty rag, all swelled up and with the blood all up in the cracks and around his fingernail and the blood wasn't even red anymore it was *black.*

He twisted a smile and pulled a long drag from his cigar, smoke flooding the table until finally his head shivered once and dropped to the side, spewing a slow leak of vomit down to the floor.

"*That's it,*" Skeet sang, giving baby pats at his back. "*That's it, let it all out...*"

And in that moment, for the first time since its conception, I was totally at peace with what we were doing. It was also maybe the only time I was fully convinced it would work; that it would go off without a hitch and finally the whole thing could be gone and forgotten, never to be thought of again. But I also realized something else.

I was hella scared.

Prentice popped up then, a string-haired jack-in-the-box sending down slaps at the table.

"*How's-about-another-round!*" he whooped. "*Egggg-hhh....*"

Skeeter scurried for the bar, his small collection of chains rattling at his waist and calling up images of eerie Christmas Eves and the undigested potato of Jacob Marley. I turned, and Prentice's eyes bulged in his face.

He was looking at Ray.

"Dude, there is a circle on your face."

"*That*," Spike said, "is ringworm."

"Oh, ringworms? I know how to get ridda ringworms. Want me to tell ya?"

"How's that?" Ray asked, half-amused.

"Well," Prentice said, "first get you a cup of vinegar. Not the white vinegar—don't get that— what you need is the *apple cider* kind. Follow?"

"Continue."

"All right, get da cup of vinegar and then lay you a *penny* in there. Now some say you get better results with a wheat penny, but I don't necessarily believe that—I think it's hogwash, actually—and most recent studies agree. But if you want to use a wheat penny, go ahead, more power to you. I would tell ya to use the quarter right there around that boy's neck, but it's gotta be copper. You under- stand, a *copper coin?*"

Ray smiled. "A copper coin."

"Soak it a day or two, then take and *lay that coin over that worm*." He leaned forward, tapping one bloodied finger at the table. "That *vinegar* does something to the *copper* that kills that *worm*."

"It's not a worm," Spike said. "It's a fungal in- fection."

"Worm, infection, whatever. But what you re- ally need is to get ya four or five cups going, put you a penny in each one—don't put more 'an one penny in each cup or it ain't gonna work."

Skeet limped over with the beers, and coming

closer I noticed a splotchy tattoo along the side of his neck. At first, I thought it was some kind of butterfly—a swastika maybe—but then I saw that what it was, it was just these two little holes with a splatter of blood coming out. Very corny.

"What's happening?"

I told him, "We're discussing fungal infections."

Skeet looked at Ray.

"Get some Barbasol shaving cream," he said, clicking his tongue. "Rub it up there every night 'fore you go to bed. Takes it right off."

Spike muttered, "Or some antifungal cream..."

"Yeah, or you could do that. Kinda *boring*, but you could do it..."

Prentice grinned and raised his beer: "*Apple. Cider. Vinegar.*"

He was gloating.

§

Later, he took us outside to see his bike.

It wasn't a big bike—wasn't a Harley or anything—but it was big in his heart, you could tell. Oh he rubbed at it, and touched it sweetly, and I suspected he drew close and whispered to it on those late nights when no one else was around. "See this," he would say, "or that," and would point to all the different parts of the motor, and tell us what they did and how he'd made this one or that one better or faster.

"That's cool, Prentice."

"Awesome."

Mostly though the bike was just this bit-and-piece custom gig: black and all dusty, with a dirt-bike sorta feel. Couple bolts short of street legal, from the looks of it, but that didn't matter as long as Prentice didn't go mowing down toddlers, ripping over mailboxes, stuff like that. There were only two cops left in town who had it out for Prentice, and both their names were mud besides.

Two, that was, until James Harrell.

Skeet's bike was a little bigger than Prentice's, and a little nicer as well, and following the official tour of each one, we stood around awhile just spitting and drinking in the alley, and again the feeling came that maybe life had changed forever. That getting the gang back together had only been trying to resurrect a bit of those glory days that were long gone and never coming back.

Old wineskins.

Afterwards we walked inside and I pushed to the wet rooms, and was dutifully greeted by the slow creak of someone having a bowel movement in the far stall. For some reason, this noise unnaturally disturbed me, and I was still reliving it moments later when I walked out and noticed a small crowd gathered near the back; following their stares, I saw Prentice slumped over our table, fists slamming hard against the wood as he tried as hard as he possibly could to *stop laughing*. Buster stood over him, a thick vein barreling down the middle of his forehead.

He was fussing at Prentice about the vomit.

Ray had grabbed a swatter and was swatting at

flies, Spike only shaking his head as finally Buster tore away from the table and huffed past me, the smell of sweat following him like a ghost. As he passed, he gave me this sort of serious look and said, "*Getcha cousin, Wes! I'm at ninety-nine, this stuff's gotta go!*"

I approached the table and Prentice peered up at me, the joy like a light in his eyes. He sprang drunkenly forward and said, "Didja pull the trigger? Huh Wes? *Didja!*"

What he meant was, when I was in the bathroom, did I make myself puke by sticking a finger down my throat...hence, "pulling the trigger." But I only stared back, no words, none at all. Buster, meanwhile, had circled the bar and was now holding a couple rags from one of the shelves.

"*Clean it up!*" he bellowed, and tossed the towels at Prentice's limp bouffant.

They fell short and swooped to the floor.

Prentice's head fell over the table and started laughing. Except for one old folks' table by the door, all conversation in the bar had stopped. Even the music seemed to have dropped a level; only the TV chattered on. Somebody yelled, "Black his eye, Buster!" and there was a small murmur of agreement.

Others told the man to shut up and breathed threats of their own.

Now Prentice was falling all over himself he was laughing so hard, and was doing this annoying thing where he just kept saying "Oh! Oh-o-oh!

Ohhhhh..." Skeet wandered over blindly, a goofy grin on his face.

And suddenly it was too much, all of it.

What small crumbs remained of my life were rotting before me, and knowing this fact brought back the deep blue sadness I'd tried so hard to forget. And then without knowing it, without ever stopping to think what I was doing, I got down on my knees, collected the rags...and started to clean.

"No!" Prentice yelped, bolting up. "Don't even mess with it, Wes!"

"*You got some nerve Cerona, laying that out in here!*" Buster wailed.

Prentice told Buster, in no uncertain terms, to go fuck himself. Then he told him to go give his ugly mother the works too—Buster just about blew a gasket when he said that. At first he kind of held on to the bar, grabbing at it like he was about to fall over; then he snatched something from under the counter and took off. Prentice and Skeet shot for the door. He was in the midst of running when all of a sudden Prentice up and busted one, a loud ripping fart that seemed to shake the walls as he tore across the bar. Buster was barely out the door when we heard the buzz of motorcycles spinning from the alley.

A moment later Buster wobbled in, still lugging the little club he'd grabbed from the bar. He was sweating like a pervert, and you could see his stomach sloshing around under his shirt from breathing so hard. His shiny black shucking glove still dangled from one hand.

"Ungrateful little shit..."

And the more I sat there scraping bile and listening to the music being buzzed by a newsbreak on TV, and people eating air about all the stupid things people eat air about in bars—the more those dark feelings swirled, showing me just how much I hated everybody and everything. Yes, I hated myself so much all I could think about was dying. Yes, life was existence in a hidden closet. And yet still I could feel Ernul's and everybody there playing me like a harp and giving me a violent hard-on and the walls closing in and shrinking like something out of a Lewis Carroll wet dream.

I knew then that I was going crazy.

Buster thanked me, but only once. He said Prentice used to bring business to this place, now all he brought was *this* crap—well, it ain't flyin'! Then he told me to tell my cousin that if he knew what was good for him, he wouldn't bring his face around there no more. That's more or less what he said, anyway. Meanwhile, Prentice had torn such terrific wind that the whole place stank of diarrhea; over at the bar, one of the Bruchac boys had grown vocal with his assessment of the situation, which consisted mostly of the phrase "Who busted the cantaloupe?" He said that about fifteen times—"*Who busted the cantaloupe?*"—his voice screeching with that last piece of puberty never fallen into place. He kept going on and on with it, laughing and fanning the air and looking around, and you could tell he really thought he was this real clever guy, saying something like who busted the cantaloupe. Right. Bill Shakespeare, everybody.

Meanwhile Ray kept swatting at flies and Spike stared into space, his head shaking back and forth and back. "*That boy...*" he would say. Said he didn't know what had come over him, just what in blazes had gotten *into* him. "I just don't *know.*" He lifted his hat and swiped a hand across his sticky forehead, and in the autumnal haze of the bar his face looked hard and miserable.

I had almost finished cleaning when Buster walked over with a cold one, propping it on the table. "This one's on the house," he said.

I started to say something, but just then somebody called his name and he walked away, the smell of sweat still trailing him like a cloud. Then I got together all the rags and tossed them away, and settling back at the table Ray was splurging details about Saturday when he would be heading south on a Greyhound bus, off to dot i's with Folsom's dredger in Louisiana. Sad days.

The three of us made plans for tomorrow night's show—it was the only appropriate thing to do, after all, before Prentice's brain was senselessly splattered up Hall's Creek Road, or his eventual incarceration for breaking James Harrell's face— and it wasn't long after when Spike got up and left, talking through yawns and jamming another half-smoked cigarette into a tray of yellowed filters. Ray and I stayed awhile longer, talking little but only gazing off at each other and across the barroom floor, minds blitzed with cheap beer and the still-strong smell of busted cantaloupe. Moe smashed Curly with a breakaway vase, and Curly appeared more aroused than infuriated. Larry, the only non-Howard brother there, looked on with intense empathy.

I laughed, a sweet hollow laughter that rang across the bar.

"*Kill 'im Curly!*" I sputtered. "*Knock his FRIG-GIN' BLOCK OFF!!!*"

Ray stepped to the bar to speak to some people he knew there—they had come in together, not long after Prentice flew the coop—and sitting alone at the booth, I caught the smallest hint of vomit still rising from the floor.

The smell followed me all the way home.

SONGS IN THE NIGHT

It was sometime after three a.m. when I woke up.
For a long time I tossed and turned, flapping the sheets and trying not to think, until finally I could take it no longer and climbed out of bed. With Ray snoring on the living room couch, I moved outside and strolled the backyard, scoping out the burn pile—now only ashes—and fiddling with the quarter still dangling bright and shiny around my neck. Nothing so special about it, no reason to dangle it on a string and parade it around like that, although growing up back in New Bern some kids had got it in their heads and somehow it had become a fad. A quarter or a shark's tooth, didn't matter. The shark's teeth came from Texasgulf, the phosphate plant over in Aurora; the quarters they blew holes

in with their daddies' rifles.

After a while things got a little mixed up in my head, though, standing around out there so late at night, and soon I started out through the pines—not knowing why, only that it needed to be done. The sky was starry and perfect above, and it wasn't long before I heard the old Norfolk Southern slinking along the rails, the soft glow of the loco-motive's headlamp glimmering around the bend; finally the train appeared, slithering mindlessly and quiet so late at night, absent of all the usual bells and whistles. And as the old freight rumbled by through the pines and the wind went rushing into our town through the valley of the frogs, my body began to rock and sway in the darkness.

It was a crazy thing to do, I know, shaking like that out in the woods in the dead of night, but I couldn't seem to help it. The moment was overwhelming, and all at once it seemed I'd spent my entire life trying to laugh down a heavy con-science; a conscience plagued by its own army of ghosts and things that go bump in the night. I'd even convinced myself I was happy because I was having fun; but that kind of fun cuts both ways, and really I was scared, alone, and lying to myself so I wouldn't actually think about who I was and be one of those people who sat around and cried all the time, dabbing at my cheeks with Kleenex and toying with thoughts of hey, maybe moving back home, turning my life around, doing something *real*. Meanwhile, back in reality, there was a sweaty fat man riding me like a greased-up pig and I was too mud-drunk to even notice.

I was miserable. I wanted to believe I was getting it right—I *needed* that, somewhere deep inside—but now things were different, were botched, and I knew it.

I pulled my Marlboros and reached inside, but instead of a cigarette this time revealed the curious black stone Ray had produced all those weeks ago. Looking closer, I noticed the sharp edge where only days earlier—as much out of terror as curiosity—I'd taken a hammer and carefully chiseled off a lip of stone. Then I'd taken the chip, poured a cold glass of water, and with sweat streaming down my face...dropped it inside.

For a moment the water only fizzled and hissed, bubbles floating to the surface. As I watched, the stone seemed to dissolve, crumbling in and in on itself, and then was gone, leaving the water a darker, tea-colored substance. And that's when I realized: it wasn't a stone. That's the shape it may've taken, but it wasn't a stone—nor was it just another drug, either. Whatever it was in that strange rock, whatever power it held, whatever mystery, in that moment I knew it wasn't merely a case of chemicals, wasn't biological, wasn't physical at all—it was *spiritual.*

It was magick.

And suddenly this was a dimension I felt I had no business tampering with.

For the first time in my life it was a dimension

that seemed unknown and unknowable, full of unseen fears and dangers at every turn. Wasn't that exactly the sort of business that had gotten Ray and Prentice into this to begin with? The same type of careless good humor on which these unutterable powers thrived? Yes, and there was no sense in playing there, no sense in tampering with that world, and yet...

And yet what would become of Prentice if nothing was done?

What should happen to him if he didn't receive this cure, this *healing* he so obviously needed?

I shuddered to think of it—much as I'd shuddered pouring that unholy concoction down the drain—but...*death*, ladies and gentleman; that was the unspoken word of the day, the elephant in the room of our own sad lives. His, mine, ours, everything seemed ripe for *death*. And if this stone had just half the answers to that conundrum, if it had even a cheap patch to preserve the problem, then it was a chance I was willing to take...

I slipped away the stone and rested on the bank, staring past the untold numbers of boxcars shifting down the line. When they had passed, I climbed up and started along the tracks, stumbling through the darkness and all the way out to Riverside and the old Arant lumber mill. Supposedly Riverside had been this nice little community back in the sixties—flowers and families and fun—but since then had lapsed into little more than a ghost town: Reelsboro County's collective cellar. People used to say the crackheads had taken over at Arant, turned it all into a bunch of crackhouses and crackwhores' dens, but I didn't see any of that.

After a quick smoke by the water I walked back and crawled into one of the old abandoned millhouses. Mostly it was empty inside, just shadows and a pile of something stacked against one wall—rotted lumber, maybe, or a dead crackhead—but I couldn't quit this feeling like I was being watched. I still wasn't feeling so hot, so I just sort of collapsed there on the floor and stared at the old millhouse roof, still fingering my quarter, still not quite sure what to make of myself. Running the proposed events of tomorrow night over and over in my head and turning them this way and that, twisting them through the great lens of wishful thinking until finally—

He won't show.

The thought struck me like a speeding bullet.

I pushed it away, my mind wrestling to go in some other—*any* other—direction...and then began to consider: what if he *doesn't* show? What if for some incalculable reason our hallowed guest decided not to come at all? What would we do for Plan B? There was no Plan B. Plan B involved death. Prentice's death. And maybe, ultimately...my own.

I needed sleep.

Needed it now, fast.

I turned on my stomach, finally dozing off and having nightmares of addicts descending madly on the mill, stumbling like starved zombies through the streets. Then they'd grabbed hold and began tearing at my flesh, ripping me apart, when suddenly I sat up and just about had a heart attack because all these ants had crawled over while I was sleeping and were eating away at my feet, and it took me forever to kick off my shoes and pick the little bastards out of my socks.

After that I'd had enough and climbed out again through the crumbling wall and back into the world, the first breath of morning burning low and bright on the horizon. Then the long journey home and walking through the door I noticed Ray still collapsed on the couch, his face a splotch in the darkness, and passing him my quarter caught the only hair of sun and for an instant was the world's smallest flashlight dangling from a hay string. Then I was in bed, branches of the old oak tapping a dark melody on the glass of my window as I shut my eyes and slowly fell off to dreams, completely ignorant of the fact that in another twenty-four hours one of us would be dead.

III: DOWNBOUND TRAIN

FRIDAY

Sometime later I woke, drenched in a greasy sweat that made much more sense as I rolled over and saw the clock faded on the night-stand, the ceiling fan stalled overhead. Just another day in paradise, I realized, and after moving down the hall and flipping the breakers, for a moment I stood watching the breath wash back into the place, the lights snapping on, the refrigerator humming to life. I noticed Ray asleep on the couch—peculiar, I thought, so late in the day—and had started back for my room when I caught the first whiff of some terrible thing that had found its way into my house.

It was coming from the bathroom.

I walked over, not really wanting to, and through the crack of the door saw something wrong with the walls, some sort of darkness. I stepped closer, pushing back the door to a picture one never wants confronting them so early in the morning—or any other time, for that matter. Sort of like that chainsaw scene in *Scarface*, only instead of blood somebody had come along and bled *shit* everywhere, all over the sink, drenching the tiles— and a bright sprawl of vomit, streaking like some cockeyed shooting star across the walls.

I flinched back, the obscene stench of it gripping me like a vise until at last I fell choking to the floor, and when I looked next Ray had wobbled over, still swaddled in his blanket from the couch.

"Ray," I said, sort of yelling, "Ray, what have you *done?*"

Only then I looked and saw the spittle caked around his mouth, the deep lavender bags beneath his eyes. He offered a lonesome stare, his yellow eyes pleading for something always out of reach— and suddenly it all hit home, all the anger crashing down as an odd sort of empathy wrapped me like a shroud. *What a douche.*

"Never mind," I finished lamely. "Just go lay down, I got it."

"No, Wes, I...I'd meant to get up, clean that mess before you ever saw it. I just..." He ran both hands down his face. "I had a bad time this morning, that's all, but I'm fine now. Really, gimme ten minutes—"

He started in.

"I told you don't worry about it," I said, forcing him back. "Just get some rest Ray, please. He's gonna be here in a couple hours and the last thing we need is you shittin' all over the place..."

We started to argue. I told him shut up and lay down, he said leave him alone, he's fine. He started in; I pushed him back. After maybe five minutes of swinging dicks I'd finally painted a convincing enough portrait of what disaster would befall us if he didn't do exactly as I said, then pushed him to my room and closed the door.

I stumbled to the bathroom, staring miserably at the mess awaiting me inside—the second mess, in fact, in twelve hours. *Lookee there, Wes, looks like you found yourself a career after all. What's the going rate, you think, for sweeping up human waste these days?*

I grabbed some towels and got to work.

§

It was slow business.

Unlike at Ernul's, Ray's leftover had not only dried but actually *hardened* into something much more sinister, an amalgam of foul deposits bottled up all morning. Even so, I'd put a fair dent in the clean-up and was still busy working away when I heard the noise from outside.

It was the clunk of a car door.

I moved to the window and saw my landlord's dually parked out front, the whole truck covered in mud. Only a few feet away stood Morty himself, belly hanging out, one hand raised to the sun as he stared across to the neighbor's yard and—

UNCLE MORT!

I ran, snatching up some random cologne and pumping it in the bathroom, then down the hall. I'd sprayed most of the kitchen when I heard the tell-tale creaks of Morty mounting the front porch and quickly hurried back, making sure to shut the bathroom door.

There were two knocks—*one two*—then the sudden jangling of keys. A moment later the door opened and Morty's huge shadow moved in over the living room carpet.

"*Helloooowww?*"

"Hello!" and I came down the hall, damp with sweat and the deep smell of musk. I was beginning to think I hadn't sprayed enough cologne.

"Howdy, Wes'n."

"How's it going, Uncle Morty?"

Morty, of course, wasn't actually my uncle; he was related to me about as much as he was to Cher. But one night last year he'd come up to me with this sheepish little grin—it made him look demented—and asked if I wouldn't, well, if I wouldn't mind calling him *Uncle* Morty. You know, one of *those* things. I didn't care. I guess I'd call him Nipplechadnezzar if it kept the rent under two hundred.

Morty snatched out his handkerchief and dabbed at his eyes. "Where ya been?"

I told him I'd been laying a turd in the bathroom.

"Mm, and I can smell it," he said, taking a breath. He glanced lazily down the hall and around the living room; more of Ray's blankets lay crumpled in a heap on the floor. Finally, he let out a breath—it sounded like *ahhhh*—and fell onto the couch.

Morty was in Vietnam. You'd never know it most of the time, but every now and again there came over him this strange sense of Armageddon, when those gray-blue eyes stared out into forever and seemed to see something there that no one else saw. Nowadays Morty lived out in the Shoals and was involved in other less-stressful activities, the most prominent of which was some sort of acting troupe that did, of all things, *medieval reenactments*. These guys, they go out dressed in aluminum foil and piggyback stallions and toss friggin' *javelins* at each other for a living (Morty was stabbed with one once out near Williamsburg). He wasn't the best landlord a person could hope for, but he wasn't the worst either.

"So," he said. "How's things?"

"Things are good," I told him, falling into my chair, playing up a smile but nodding my head seriously. "Got a few good leads on some jobs, you know, think I'll check those out. Momma's birthday's next week. Other than that, it's just been the same old...same old stuff."

"Same old song and dance, huh?"

"That's right."

Morty laughed and got up. My heart floated as for one terrible moment I thought he'd turn left, down the hall. Instead, he revealed a tape measure and walked slowly to the kitchen, taking measurements for the new stove hood he'd been promising since last December.

We talked. At first about the hood, and how much better the place would look with it, then about how he was still going to come down one afternoon and haul off that old fridge on the back porch, that he hadn't forgotten me. Then he started asking about the microwave he'd given me when I first moved in, just so I wouldn't think he was a total prune. And the whole time he was there I kept farting and saying things like, "I told you this place needs fumigatin'—you hear those barking spiders? Ya *smell* that?" And then Morty'd say "Whoo-ee boy, you are *rotten*."

I had turned on the TV, not because I wanted to watch anything but so there wouldn't be total silence while Morty worked, and so there would be something to muffle the sound when Ray inevitably fell off the bed. There wasn't much on but a lousy football game, though.

"What happened to your timer here?" he asked, tapping the stove clock. "You always have this thing blinking like that?"

"Power went out. Hadn't got around to it."

He started pressing buttons. "How's that cousin of yours? Hain't heard much from him lately."

You knew it, Wes, you knew it was coming. It always does...

"He's good," I said.

"He playing tonight?"

"Yuh. Far as I know."

"I figured he was, mm-hmm." Morty jostled out his pad, scribbling something. "I hear that Harrell boy got out of the hospital last week. You know that?"

"Nah, I didn't know that, Uncle Morty."

"Yep," he said, and drew the word out— *yuuuuuuppp*—so that he sounded kind of bored or dumb.

I was getting worried. I was getting worried that if Morty stuck around long enough his bladder might get the hiccups. He'd head for the bathroom, and of course I'd have no choice but to tackle him to the ground. There would be a struggle. In the end, he would spend the rest of his days in bloody pieces, rotting in the old fridge out back, Mortimer Whitfield: the ultimate purloined letter. So whenever it looked like he was moving away from the kitchen, I'd walk over and start messing with the TV—fiddling with the Brightness and Tint, positioning the ears, eycing my VHS collection of Vincent Price/Bela Lugosi fan favorites. And every time I'd show some serious plumber's crack, 'cause I'd poke my little butt out like a whore so it was all sticking out and hanging in the hall. Then I'd go back to my seat and start cutting some more whoppers.

Too much more of this and I'll start crying, I thought crazily. *I mean it. I'll weep.*

For much, I figured I'd die right there in that chair and no one would ever know just how lonely

I was before I died. And yet I could see it clearly, could see myself just sort of floating away from everyone I'd ever known and all of them waving back at me and sobbing as I floated farther and farther away, blowing them all kisses and with this really tired look on my face and the feeling that—

The tape measure snapped shut.

Morty jotted the last of the measurements into his pad, let out a breath, and stepped triumphantly away from the stove. Suddenly I could make out the sound of Ray's snores bowling down the hall; I cranked the TV and cheered.

"Oh, yeah," Morty said, "almost forgot to tell you. The Movement's helping out with an event this Wednesday."

"Oh?" That's what they called their little performance group: The Movement.

"Yeah, down your neck of the woods, matter fact—New Bern?"

"Is that right?"

"That's right. We're doing the Battle of New Bern?" Morty snickered. "What is it Wes'n, whatcha got that look on your face fors?"

"What are you doing getting mixed up in the Civil War, Uncle Mort?"

"I said the *saaaaame* thing, but this is through the *Historical Society*, m'boy. Large sums of money we're talking here." You had to love the way he said that—*large-sums-a-money*—like it was all one word or something. Boy, what a sellout. Morty had zero passion for the Civil War, but I guess anybody'll go out and play dead for the right price; hell, Morty'd probably go around wearing a tutu and toting a bazooka if some *historical society* paid him enough to do it. I'd already known about the event anyway, had found a flyer in the mailbox. I figured Morty'd put it there.

"It's a collaboration with the North-on-South Troupe," he said, wiping the sweat from his eyes. "Now they do *scripted battle reenactments*, you see, and not just the performances like we do. There's a difference."

He was right. When I was a kid, my father had once tried taking us to see the Battle of New Bern. I can still remember the drive out to the fields, before the storm landed and the rains came down. Remember Dad telling me how true-to-history the whole thing was and what kinds of things these guys did to make it look just right; how they all played real-life people and how the people who really died would still die, and all the people who lived would still live—they'd *always* still live—and how all the weapons were right on the money, and even how they all urinated on the buttons they wore so the things would look old. He didn't tell me what they did to the uniforms.

Morty ripped a page from his pad.

"You should come on out next Wednesday," he said.

But I was pretending to watch the game.

He dabbed his face once more with his handkerchief and then finally started for the door, not getting far when he stopped suddenly and grabbed at his pockets, as if he'd forgotten something that went there.

"Now, didn't you say you were having some kind of...an issue there with the toilet bowl?"

"Mm?"

"A problem with the commode? A bad flapper, uh?"

A quick pain up one leg. Nausea. But I only smiled like old times and shook my head, squinting my eyes in grim appraisal. Somebody once told me I looked like James Dean when I did that; then this other girl had to go and ruin it and say he doesn't look like James Dean, he looks like *Leonid Breshniv.*

"It's good," I said, and smiled. "Toilet's fine, Morty."

I didn't mention the leak under the sink.

§

Ray was sleeping when I brought in some water, so after leaving the glass next to the bed I went and grabbed some sheets from the hall and covered him, hanging another from the window to block out the light.

Then I finished with the bathroom.

Afterwards I showered and spent the next few hours cleaning around the house: tidying the kitchen, taking out the trash, doing some laundry. Once finished, I checked the clock and went to the fridge, reaching far back for the sixer of Bud I'd put there days earlier. Grabbed one and took it out.

Without thinking much about what I was doing, I pulled the small stone from my pocket, setting it on the counter. Very slowly, very carefully, I twisted the cap and reached for the stone—trying harder not to think now, to blank my mind of all memory, all intellect, all emotion—and held it in my palm, watching the way it seemed to flicker and gleam in the early evening light.

I dropped it inside.

Just as with the water a week earlier, the beer began to bubble and pop. Suds rose fiercely, threatened to overflow, and then sank to nothing, and in the next moment all was quiet and the brew appeared every bit as harmless as before...if perhaps only a shade darker. I reapplied the cap, jamming it into a fix on the bottle, and stood away, eyeing the abominable creation. And it was good.

As a final touch I bent forward, peeling back the smallest corner of the bottle's wrapper and then, with the care of one handling an atomic bomb, placed the beer back into its cardboard holster and closed the refrigerator door.

I checked the time and considered waking Ray, finally deciding to wait and give him another twenty, thirty minutes. He would need it. Finally, I grabbed a beer—my own, of course, careful to avoid the bullet in Ray Lafargue's twisted version of Russian Roulette—and moments later after settling on the porch, I wondered what it might take to get through the night. And would it all really be as easy as Ray made out? I tried pretending it was, like the whole thing had played out just like the Civil War, like everything had already happened was now set in stone. Saw it all happen, right before my eyes: saw our man taking the beer and knocking it back, gulping it down like the thousands of beers he'd gulped all his life, the (*magic*) moving like liquid through his mind, opening doors that had been locked and lost for centuries.

We produce the ecstasy...

Saw our walk to Prentice's and everything waiting when we got there: a writhing mass of humanity, all eyes fogged over with a furtive mix of pleasure and pain as their bodies glistened in candlelight. Then the slow thundering of a drum, deep and subterranean, full of hell's fury.

We provide the trance...

Prentice emerged on stage. He grabbed the mike with both hands and screeched over the crowd, voice raw and cracking and near death, the voice of a dying man calling out.

And then we wait...

We stood over him in darkness, his pale form collapsed in a corner of his room, and then only silence as two hands—*his* hands—were moving in the night, searching, attaching themselves to my cousin. They began to glow...

§

But then I opened my eyes and the first thing I noticed was the eerie way the sun seemed to have vanished over the horizon. My beer had turned over, and was still dripping down into the porch when I snatched it up and hurried inside and back to my room, giving Ray a few hard shakes before a funny feeling made me stop and notice the awkward form of his body beneath the sheets. There was something uncivilized in that rest—something *vulgar*, and primitive—and pulling back the sheets, I quickly understood why.

His skin was faded, giving up its usual tan in lieu of a pale gray that made him inexplicably less human, not of this world. The scar remained over his chest, fat and swollen but still with that lavender touch—and yet it was in his *eyes* where the true misery resided, no longer brown but now hopelessly black and faded.

They were looking at me.

"It's them..." he mumbled, a whisper from beyond. *"They're killing me..."*

For a moment I said nothing, watching in grim fascination as the tangled mass rose and fell over his heart. "Who, Ray? *Who's* killing you?"

"I wasn't...wasn't meant to tell anybody about that deal," he whispered. "They told me I'd die a horrible death if I did, a death worth a thousand deaths. But nobody runs forever—you know that don't you?—and neither could I. And then *Prentice...*"

A single tear slipped down his cheek, past the neat white circle of his ringworm and then vanishing beneath the fuzzy maze of his beard. Ray stared at me, his eyes sliding back and forth in his skull until I recognized in them every nightmare I'd ever hoped to never come true, a reflection bruised by scenes of degradation and horror, of madness filling the earth with a great harvest of murder and war and—

"You're not dying," I told him, hoping it was true. "You're just sick, you've—"

His thin arm reached out, grabbing me roughly and pulling me close.

"I'm *dying*," he breathed, mouth yawping to say more when suddenly there came a knocking, a gentle tapping from down the hall. Ray groaned miserably, his pale hand dropping from my arm as I went and pulled back the blanket over the window, looking out.

"It's him," I said. "He's here."

Ray stared at me, eyes whirling with some uncertain misery.

"*What about...?*"

The sentence hung in the air, and when the silence was complete I turned and walked out of the room, shutting the door and then starting down the hall toward those still, soft knocks at the door. And only then did I notice another, much subtler sound, a sudden rush overhead.

It was the sound of rain.

A million thoughts as I moved to the door and made ready for what awaited me on the other side, tangled notions of healing and hope spinning in a mad corkscrew through my mind. Memories of Prentice collapsed across our booth the night before, and of Buster screeching from on high. Of sad James Harrell, the first whipping boy of this new and darker nature, and of Ray and Taco and—

—and finally memories of Spike himself, shuffling in from the porch and the gentle hooves of the rainfall beyond. We traded a few playful jabs as he came in and strolled the living room, studying the walls and putting his finger to Dalí's *Rose Meditative* and *Metamorphosis of Narcissus*. He paused to give a gentle shake to the empty bottle I'd spilled on the porch.

"Getting started early, ain't you, bud?"

I laughed and told him I was, playing for casual but falling short. Then I went to the fridge and grabbed a bottle from inside, handed it over.

"One for the road," I told him.

Spike received the beer with a smile, and in doing so a great weight was lifted off my chest.

Next to him not showing up, my next biggest fear had been Spike casually waving the bottle aside, not in the mood. That hadn't happened, and for another of those fleeting moments I caught the notion that this might actually work.

He fell to the couch, taking that same breath Morty had taken only hours earlier, that slow seepage of life through the mouth. He said, "Heard much from Ray?"

And subtly I began sliding the quarter back and forth around my neck, the calling of a genie that just wasn't there. "He stopped by to say he'd be with Keri until late, that he'd meet us at the show sometime tonight." I let out this real obnoxious snort when I said it, like it was totally obvious Ray and Keri had to go and have this whole ton of sex or something before he left.

"Keri Scott?"

"Yep."

Spike laughed. "Well, he better spend some time with that baby of his, he knows what's good for him—if Keri'll let him. Ray's been jumping states all year chasing money, spent all summer trying to buy that wreck off Stick Folsom. Now he's looking to go *back* down south tomorrow?" He laughed again, an unimpressed tee-hee-hee. "Sometimes, tell you the truth, I wonder why she has anything to do with him..."

Instead of thinking I only moved to the kitchen, snatching a beer of my own from the holster and swallowing half. Outside the rain had picked up, thundering now at the roof, and with it that stone-cold depression came sweeping again over my soul.

It won't stop, I thought with horror. *It'll rain all evening and all night and we'll be trapped in this house forever.* Then I thought of Ray back there, probably puking his little heart out, blowing snot all over the sheets and cussing imps and ogres and grogs, oh my.

No sooner had it started, however, than suddenly the rain let up, the sun peeping through for one final bow before sunset. Spike sat up, peering at me through those two great lenses.

"That's our cue," he said. "Better get a move on, before it really starts pouring."

I agreed and hurried down the hall, checking my look in the mirror as I slipped into my belt and threw on a few heavy squirts of cologne. I did these things automatically and without much thought, and yet...and yet on another level—a level not observed with human eyes—that dark, separate part of me rejoiced. I suppose there had still been that piece of me, leftover from the night before, perhaps, that still believed Spike wouldn't come. But he had, he *had* come, and was presently down the hall sipping a beer just as he'd done a thousand times before...only this beer was different. This beer had spunk, had *pizzazz*. This beer would blow your hair right on back—and then blow your mind.

And suddenly I felt horrible, a traitor in disguise. The emotion was not a new one; I'd come to know it well, in fact, grappling with the bitch of it vigorously over the past three weeks. Because no matter how I twisted the setup, no matter which way it was turned, I'd never be at peace with the specifics of the situation (*don't you mean conspiracy?*), the way we were using Spike, manipulating him— or some terrible, clandestine part of him—against his knowledge, doing no less than slipping him the mystic equivalent of a Mickey Finn. No, worse than that: we were *poisoning* him. We were gambling with death and magic, and Spike was our primary chip.

But just as this emotion was a well-known one, so was the mechanism that now slid it away, tucking it neatly and without mess back into the box from which it had crawled.

Nice, neat box.

When I came out Spike was laid across the couch, finally standing and slipping into his hat while I went and grabbed up my beer from the kitchen, took another long swig. Spike met this with a swig of his own and was almost to the door when I noticed the bottle in his hand. Really looking at it this time, at the tell-tale wrapper and the way it seemed to have come back together on the bottle. Like brand-new.

Hm.

Then a fuzzy feeling, creeping sickly like a sap up my throat; I glanced down, staring at the bottle in my own brittle hands, the slow curl of the wrapper burning itself into my brain and causing a low sort of grumbling deep in my stomach. I staggered back, not understanding and understanding completely, my world suddenly falling away as the tragic mix-up and all its implications rushed out to meet me, to shake hands and say *how do you do?*

Something fluttered in my stomach; first hope, then—more powerful—*fear*.

"Wes? You ready?"

I stumbled away, back and back and back down the hall and falling into the bathroom, slamming the door. Collapsing to the toilet and taking firm hold of the bowl, embracing it as I'd done so many, many nights before...

And pulling the trigger.

Then it came, rising up and bursting out of me in a great mud-colored tide, and when it was done I said not good enough and returned to the well, gagging myself a second time. Finally, I stood to my feet, and had started out when I glanced up and saw in my reflection a form that was more shadow than substance, eyes gulped in darkness and mouth slivering a wry grin that was utterly not of this world. For a moment I stared at the image, those endless black eyes searching my own until at last I turned away, trying to forget, trying to move on and find that nice, neat box as I opened the door and saw the hallway clouded with fog, thin layers of it swirling in eddies from the floor.

"Everything okay down there, bud?"

I noticed Spike at the end of the hall, a distant, cockeyed silhouette, and for some reason seeing him there in all that fog sort of gave me the creeps and so I only mumbled something and kept down the hall, not wanting to look at what was happening around me, not wanting to see it at all.

I stumbled to my room, flung back the door and was met with more of that same ethereal fog, still dancing, still swirling as I fell inside and...

And then I saw Ray.

His eyes bulged enormously from his face, two perfect windows of terror and awe and some hidden wisdom as they peered to the ceiling, lost in a plane of some other existence. He was panting, his small French lips parted in a rictus as terrible as the boils sprouting now like spoiled daisies over his chest, slowly covering the scar.

He reached out, one hand gripping roughly at my own and pulling me close until at last a sudden fire swept up my arm, my shoulder, sinking down into my heart; I pushed back, struggling to free myself and Ray only holding tighter as tiny blisters rose and popped up his neck and then, suddenly, I realized what was happening.

The burning...

"Where are you, Ray? Come back, please, I need you..."

But Ray only groaned, his eyes gleaming darkly and face swallowed in tears, smoldering away as they slid down his ruby-red cheeks; his ringworm glistened sickly beneath one eye.

He leaned forward, struggling to pull himself up when the last of the sheets came tumbling down and I saw the bed beneath covered in flies—many of them dead, some still buzzing weakly as Ray sank deeper into the mattress.

I yanked my arm free.

Stumbled back through the fog, the tears still streaming brightly down his face.

The clock flashed, casting its cool red glow across the room, and with dawning horror I watched as my surroundings pulsed and writhed to life—melting, changing, morphing. A blink of the eyes, and suddenly all light was gone as the bed, the window, the wall, everything began to shadow in on itself, caving in, going dark, until only the numbers remained.

11:34

11:34

All notions of Ray had vanished, replaced with the knowledge of some powerful presence sweeping the room. Then came terror as I sensed the floor dropping, falling away from me, and heard the gentle whir as it slid away like a scared animal through the night. I stretched my legs at where the floor used to be, down and down—but there was nothing there: I was floating, blindly and impossibly *floating*, suspended over indefinite fathoms of nothingness.

11:34

11:34

Now the numbers themselves had tilted, slowly twisting and turning.

They're growing, I thought, not quite believing the words—and yet, moving closer through the darkness, the digits visibly swelled, first to the size of my head, then my chest. And as they floated closer and closer to where I was, something unseen in the blackness below began groping at my legs—yanking, scratching—but then why was I not surprised, why was that feeling so expected, so *familiar*…

Only then did I glance up to see the numbers still twisting, still turning, until all at once everything spun to a silent calm.

hE:LL

hE:LL

hE:LL

And then I was falling.

§

Down and down, hurdling recklessly through space and everything dark as the wind swept past me. Too many thoughts—none of them making sense—as I plunged faster and faster into the deep, gathering speed, finally landing with a loud *crunch* that was actually my leg snapping, my arm being crushed. My heart skipped, the breath punched from my lungs.

What's going on here, Wes? Just what is this? Think!

But I couldn't think, couldn't concentrate, could barely breathe through the pain and terrible sense of loss. Blurry half-colors formed and then broke off, sinking before my eyes; a line from Ambrose Bierce floated crazily into my head: *the intellectual part of his nature was already effaced; he had power only to feel, and feeling was torment…*

I gasped for breath, mind racing as I glanced around and started to call out—for Ray, for Spike, for anybody—when some other, shrewder part of myself rose up and told me to keep my filthy mouth shut. Whatever was happening here, it said, whatever this was, the old rules had changed and suddenly I had a bad feeling I'd better learn the new ones before it was too late.

Following several timeless seconds, I realized I was lying on a level of packed earth—dirt so thin it could rightly be called sand. I was naked, somehow, and looking down noticed that my knees had been smeared with blood; I dipped my fingers down only to find the blood had dried, becoming no more than a powdery crust over my legs.

Glancing up, I could make out a soft light only yards away, glimmering along the arch of a large opening in the earthen wall; another yawned silently to my left—this one without the light—and I realized I'd landed in something like a *tunnel*, a tunnel through an immense underground cavern.

An underground cavern, eh? That's swell, Wes, only

you're no Indiana Jones, and something tells me this is not the place of happy endings, not at all.

He had power only to feel, and feeling was torment…

And then it hit me: *the stone.*

Of course, that's what it was—the fog, the darkness, the long fall through forever—everything happening like it was real but really it was the *stone*, some dark magic that was meant for Spike only now it was working through *me*, calling up fantasy and fear and the dementia of a death-obsessed mind, and maybe if I focused and concentrated hard enough and tried to—

Something moving, a scuttling off through the darkness.

I turned, staring as the firelight lapped softly from the rounded arch of the cavern, from that twisting tunnel in the distance.

Almost inviting...

I stumbled to my feet, feeling carefully through the darkness when suddenly a figure emerged, crashing to his knees in the shadows ahead; for an instant the man's gaze locked with mine, the dark pearls of his eyes revealing things there was no earthly reason I should know. Like me, he was naked, and though I'd never seen this person in my life, I suddenly knew things about him there was no earthly way I could've known.

That he'd died only twelve minutes earlier, for instance. That he had two kids; one dreamed of someday becoming a professional ball player, the other he feared was developmentally challenged.

He was born June 2, 1954, and had died in a freak electrical accident; while working, a wire had went hot and filled his body with over 10,000 volts of electric current. Surprisingly, he also had a habit of kidnapping blonde kids and collecting their heads in a hole beneath the back porch—only after molesting them, of course, something he'd been hard at since his wild college days of yore.

These thoughts came all at once, though I had no idea how, or even why.

They did not come by way of some mystical vision, were not a psychic experience, but merely cold hard fact; something I also knew to be a terrible yet natural occurrence in this place *(oh this place this place, what is this place?)*. I withdrew from him, scrambling away when I noticed the wall—at least, what I *thought* was the wall—beginning to move and twist behind the man's back. My throat struggled for words, then clenched completely as this living shadow settled over the man's ruined body, driving something deep into the pit of his back.

The man collapsed, sending small puffs of dirt into the air. He was screaming.

Suddenly the shadow began to morph and swell, reaching higher and higher, growing to a height of nine feet, and then growing more. The shroud of darkness vanished, falling piece by piece, and then his form appeared, complete with grotesquely fat legs and two mantis-like arms that dropped to uneven lengths past his gut. It was one of these limbs—the longer of the two—which now grabbed the man, scooping him over one spiky shoulder. An odd clicking sound that was meant to be laughter emitted from the creature's head. And as the beast lurched over the soil and toward the opening in the far wall, his face shone in the dull light.

And one hand clasped my mouth to keep from screaming.

Bulging insectan eyes studied wisely the outside world as shards of jagged teeth poked from an oversized jaw, the lower shelf protruding several inches beyond that of the upper. Two ears curled at random from a knobby, boil-covered skull. But what lay within the eyes was the worst, for these were nothing more than pools of living black slime; there was nothing but death in those eyes, nothing but cold evil and hate. Only the pupils shone in the darkness, two cream-colored pinpoints in a sea of black sludge.

He was still shuffling from the cavern when suddenly it was too much, and my bowels emptied themselves with ferocious force. The refuse withered in the intense heat, and I knew that this would be one of my final bowel movements of all time.

Then he was gone and for a long time I only lay there, shaking uncontrollably, I don't know for how long. Time had lost all meaning in this place, in this place there *was* no time: eternity stretched before me, and for the second time in my life I could actually grasp it, could actually fathom such concepts as timelessness and immortality.

Again I struggled to my feet, my leg still pulsing from the fall, not quite as bad as before but
enough to realize there was no healing in this place;
my arm, my leg, my wrist, they were all broken,
and they'd always *be* broken. I staggered down the
tunnel toward the arch, toward the soft effulgence
on the other side, and getting there suddenly froze
as I gazed across an immense underground cavern.

I could see for miles.

Fires blazed wildly, burning in every direction—big fires and small fires and fires that shim-
mered white against the total blackness of the
cavern. In the distance, great billows of smoke
hurled skyward, raining a storm of ash like sinister
snowfall over the rocky cavern floor. And still the
screaming, everywhere, a chorus of howls that lent
chaos to the air.

My mind rushed ahead me, sprinting in too
many directions at once, a dizzy feeling washing
over me as I remembered all the things I'd been
told about a place much like this, about a hell where
the sinners were purged forever with fire.

Don't go there, Wes, just don't even go there, this isn't—

But there was no energy for that, no energy to
sit and discuss, to debate and deal.

That was gone now—up in smoke as they say,
ha-ha—and now there was only this dark place of
death. Call it what you want, Wes, call it life's last
holiday, paid for on the tab of Murphy's Law.

You're dreaming.

You're dreaming and you'll wake up any minute now,

sweaty for sure, probably with a hangover and the feeling that you're falling from a high high place and—

But I wasn't dreaming.

I wasn't dreaming and I knew it, and yet my mind rattled on ahead of me, lying to itself to cope with this new set of circumstances (*and hey, now there's a name for it, not the Bad Place at all but just some New Set of Circumstances. I like that. That has a nice ring to it, don't you think, Wes?*).

But I couldn't think about that.

Suddenly all the problems I was having back in life seemed so distant and trivial. All the pain, the frustration, the plans I'd made, it all seemed so brisk and blissful compared with this. I wanted out—*now*—and would've easily cut my own throat to get it…but I couldn't, and I knew it. No matter how hard I tried, I knew I would never get out: there was no hope anymore, no hope for anything. It was all over now, there would be no more plans, no parties, no peace.

I would be in this place forever.

The thought brought me to my knees, and staring out over this vast arena of suffering my spirit was finally broken within. I'd started to sort of sob, hating myself for it, the tears barely shed before being scooped up by the heat. Finally, an even stranger sensation fell over me, the pain vanishing suddenly in my leg and fingers and wrist. My body rose to its feet, though I was no longer the one controlling it, and began moving down the steep hillside toward the fires below.

Realizing what was happening, I struggled to turn back—to run and hide—but it was no use: my body was being *used*, propelled to what would surely be my own death, and there was nothing I could ever hope to do about it. Moving farther down the slope, I noticed what appeared to be small branches blowing within the fires on the cavern floor, each fire raging from a chasm dug deep into the earth. Approaching one of these chasms I looked down, peering inside, and saw something I immediately wished I hadn't.

Inside this simple hole in the ground—a hole big enough to drop a backyard grill into—was a human being, their skin flaky and burned, with small slivers of flesh peeling from the bone. Grungy rats and many-legged spiders crawled along these flaps, and I noticed worms eating into flesh and infested in bone, yet none were burned by the flames washing overtop. The entire frame was absent of hair, and only by the remaining lumps of skin at her chest could I tell that she was a woman. She had been beautiful once, a queen of her tribe—I knew this, somehow—but she had also been wicked, ruthless beyond compare, and now her beauty had been marred with ashes. And as she held the tattered bones of her hands out to me, heaving maniacally back and forth within the hole, I turned, almost falling head over heels into another chasm not far from the first.

Inside this hole stood a new form, covered in splotches of dark and dried blood.

One leg was missing, and the skin had been stripped from the other so that only the shaky bone remained. This man's greatest claim to fame was that he'd once shared a dance with a young Ginger Rogers—*my swanky American lay*, he liked to call her. But only in some of those stories did they end up sleeping together on the starlet's lavatory sink; in others making out on a couch little removed from the ballroom floor. All the stories were lies, of course, except for the dance itself, which was real enough. He'd been a great politician in his day, well-respected, but what the citizens of his country weren't aware of was the countless millions he'd swindled for himself, living in luxury while they suffered under the promise of a better tomorrow.

His face turned up to mine, and I saw that in place of his eyes were two great holes in the man's head, each rimmed with blood and filled with some kind of sticky black goo. Explosions of fire swept up his frame, sending him wobbling on his one good leg, and though there's no way he could've seen me standing there, he lifted his bony hands, pleading with me in a language I did not understand.

I stumbled back in horror and, gazing out over the rocky cavern, saw hundreds more of these chasms the way one would look into the night sky and see a thousand stars. And then my body was moving, again regardless of my own will or wishes, being pushed out of the cavern and into a corridor of solid black stone. Small torches lit the walls, making them glisten and shine. A herd of rushing swine came squealing past in the dark, the flames showing dimly off their muddied pig-flesh as they pooled around me and kept forward through the darkness.

They stampeded on, their squeals fading as I hobbled farther down the blackened corridor and through a web of passages that soon opened to reveal another, much larger cavern. Staring higher, my eyes were drawn to a dark construction of bars along the cavern walls—an ominous patchwork that appeared at once cold and brutish and so black it seemed to shine in the darkness, circling in a great spiral up and up and up; I squinted as the fortress vanished through a gray mist overhead.

Whatever this was, whatever figment my mind had dreamed up (*only it's not a dream and you know it*), I decided then and there that I wanted no part. I stumbled back, retreating once more to the blackened stone corridor when a hand laid itself warmly on my shoulder, and turning I saw—

Marcelle, her eyes shining blue as the summer sky and skin gleaming golden-soft against the night. She was naked, just as I'd wanted her all those weeks ago, only now here she was, Marcelle, Marcelle, as she should've been all along.

"Wes..." she breathed, and suddenly things didn't seem so bad after all.

Not a dream, Wes, not a dream at all, but a fantasy...

"Wes, I've been waiting for you...been waiting

so long..."

I reached out, taking hold of one brilliant golden breast, so soft beneath my fingers. I cupped it fully, the nipple perking in my palm as Marcelle moved closer, pressing her body to my own.

"Been waiting so long..." she said, speaking through a sigh. *"So long to...to have you...to feel you inside me...to feel your skin being ripped from its bones..."*

My heart stopped cold in my chest.

I looked at her then, staring deep into her eyes as the pair of would-be blues eroded suddenly to swirling holes of sludge, as two withered ears curled from a boil-covered skull.

My mouth opened to scream, only creaked unsurely.

"To open your throat and bleed you like a swine..."

I stared helplessly as she reached out and grabbed hold of my arm, and with one powerful tug yanked the skin off from the elbow down. I howled, the agony ripping like fire up my arm and turning my body to one tremorous muscle while the thing snarled, releasing a deep clicking sound—more of that eerie laughter I'd witnessed earlier. A rancid smell filled the air, the swirling holes that were once her eyes brimming now with tiny maggots from their sockets, an endless deluge as clumps of the larvae fell dripping to the dusty cavern floor...

The creature reached out again with an ancient hand, this time taking hold of my chest. The nails dug in. But I only trembled, eyes lost in the great flood of worms from the monster's face and waiting in horror for that long and final tear, that terrible rending of flesh from flesh and skin from bone until—

Until Spike grabbed my arm and pulled me away.

"*C'mon*," he said, dragging me close to the cavern wall, and looking back I saw only a swirling black mist that fluttered once and then was gone. I raised my arm, expecting the worst—only now the pain, the blood and gore, all of it was gone.

My arm was fine.

Spike wandered ahead through the darkness, stopping at another of those twisted ledges running a spiral along the cavern walls. Together we mounted the steps, moving higher and higher until, glancing down, the fires glowed like a thousand burning coals below. I looked left and saw somber black bars, realizing suddenly that they were cells—not fixed within a frame but chiseled crudely within the earthen walls themselves. Each hole had been fitted with a set of dusty bars and a dirtied cell door, and dangling in an iron lump from each of the doors I noticed a padlock that looked as old and bleak as time itself.

Sort of like...like...

Like a prison.

I looked, and within the cells observed an endless series of washed-out forms, human bodies stripped naked and their flesh glimmering in the darkness as softer, paler version of themselves.

Their heads were full of worms.

Slithering in eye sockets and dangling in skeins from downturned nostrils, falling in small writhing clumps from their ears. I watched them pass, wondering who these people were and what they might've done to end up here, finally getting my answer as Spike stopped suddenly outside a shadowed cell. Without really wanting to, I turned, peering past the ominous black lock, past the bars, into the cell...

And saw Prentice.

Like the others he stood naked, his skin pale and appearing almost translucent against the darkness. Once-signature locks fell limply around his neck, now no more than a dark moss atop the stump of his frame, worms writhing in an endless tangle over his eyes as he stood dazed and empty and lost, now only waiting for death to catch up and for whatever was left of Prentice-in-life to come and join him in this place.

Forever...

NO!NO!NO!NO!NO!

My mind screamed, would've forced my eyes to switch and suddenly see someone else, to somehow make this something other than what it was—but couldn't. There was no more denying— not now, not ever again—and gazing at his pallid apparition, I finally realized: *it was false hope.* I saw that now with unusual clarity, how vain and futile it all was. Only Prentice could make the decision to change his life, and I felt like a sincere moron to think otherwise, as if we could conjure some twisted sort of shortcut. I had allowed the whole scheme—with its promises of hope and survival and of a life returned to normal—to blind me to this simple truth.

Without wanting to, I realized the dark path my own life had taken. Saw the glowing of its artificial lights, powered by pleasure and pride, and walked step after careless step down its shadowy terrain—a walk that sprawled across the years. At last I had placed ecstasy on the pedestal it had sought all along: a raging idol that strapped me to the altar of my own pride, that sad, laughable, passing pride of life. For years I'd bowed to its force, gladly succumbing to the glossed-over bacchanals I'd come to adore and that made everything so spontaneous and exciting, a life of loud music and smoke-filled rooms and everybody talking at once; of casual love and fresh faces and an ever-expanding Rolodex of merrymakers and mist-filled memories.

What I'd found was a life that rarely dealt the fantasies it inspired, complete with detours into humanity's basest desires: a mad circus of cheats and liars, and new ways of pulling it off and getting had. Like most things in life, in the end I'd gotten exactly what I paid for, my life denigrated to nothing more than a race of chemically-dependent existence, Exhibit A in some sad exposé of the human condition. I'd been walking this road a long, long time, and knew it well, and after so many miles could honestly say all I really wanted was to be left alone and be filled with hate because everybody sucked.

He will die. Prentice will die.

I knew that now, understood it deep within myself.

He would die and everybody would go to his funeral and harp about what a swell bastard he was and how if only we could all be a little bit more like the P-man, bless his departed soul…

I stepped closer, staring through the bars as the worms twisted and writhed, gleaming in the darkness.

"Sorry, man," I whispered. "I should've been there for you, should've *helped*…" Prentice twitched, glowing in the earthen cell. "*Why'd you have to go and get all stupid for, anyway?*"

Spike walked over, dropping a gentle hand on my shoulder.

"It's not your fault, Wes…"

And I knew it wasn't.

But that didn't change the feeling inside, and once more that old depression swooped down, laying its gray, calloused fingers over my soul. I dropped my head, staring over the endless horror below. The chorus of wails rose higher, the sorrow seeping now like a poison through my veins when suddenly the falling ash was cut by a brilliant light dappling from above. As I watched, the light grew brighter, piercing the mist and darkness and splashing in golden brilliance over the ledge.

Then sudden movement and I turned, watching as the ancient knot of the padlock over Prentice's door trembled once and clanged to the floor. The cell door swung open, and staring inside I watched the worms dripping in a wet freefall from Prentice's eyes. Then that radiance shone brighter, breaching inside and spreading over him, and the worms fell away, brimming from his ears and nostrils and running from his sockets until finally his own dark eyes appeared and glanced around, taking in the craggy earthen walls, the bars, the swung-wide door.

And still the light poured down, shimmering over the cavern until a second crash exploded down the ledge, and another of those ancient locks—this one from the cell directly next to Prentice's—dropped in a shower of sun-colored sparks. The door creaked slowly open, and into this glorious display of power and light and love stepped Ray Lafargue, his eyes no longer dark but full of dreadful wonder as they peered up and up and for one everlasting moment all was still, a mournful silence made complete as the ash rained its dark snowfall over the cavern, the brilliance shining still brighter from above and cascading soft and warm over my face until—

Until then I opened my eyes and was on my back in a bed of grass, staring into the glare of an endless afternoon sun.

I pulled myself up, all the horrors of that other world slowly vanishing away, replaced now with the familiar oaks and pines of my own backyard. For a long time I lay there, the images fading as if from a faraway dream and the birds chirping sweetly from the trees until finally I staggered to my feet and back to the house, and stepping inside found Spike curled up asleep on the couch. Looking a lot, I thought, like Ray had looked only twenty-four hours earlier.

Ray...

I crept quietly down the hall, pausing outside my closed bedroom door. Wondering if I really wanted to know what was on the other side, and knowing I had no choice.

Then I took a deep breath, and stepped inside.

The bed was empty, and for a moment I stood gazing at its emptiness, at the peppering of flies across its sheets and the tired, sunken look of the mattress. Sunlight shone in through the window—the blanket had been torn down, folded on a shelf near the door—and there on the nightstand I noticed the glass of water I'd brought into this room a long, long time ago.

The glass was empty.

I went and peeled out of my clothes, stopping suddenly as I caught a whiff of something and, looking down, realized at some point during the night I'd somehow managed to shit myself, the remains caked hard to my tighty-whities. I bundled the clothes, not thinking much about it, then climbed into the shower and for a long time stood savoring the rush of the warm, cleansing water against my face. Spike was still sleeping when I came out, and remained that way while I put on some coffee—needing it, hoping it would stop the shaking in my arms, the whimpers, the small clattering of teeth as they bounced in my jaw.

Then the sky turned gray and I took to staring from windows, watching as storm clouds gathered and then plowed like huge unanchored ships across the sky. I'd watch the darkness ebb and then take another sip of joe, sometimes glancing over to study the subtle rise and fall of Spike's stomach on the couch—up and down, up and down, a dependable rhythm—until finally he pulled himself up, rubbing his eyes as he saw me sitting there sipping my cup. I offered him some coffee, but Spike only waved it away, said no thanks, he wasn't in the mood. He looked at me then, a veiled sadness welling in his eyes as he nodded slowly, as if fitting together some peculiar puzzle in his head.

Finally, he stood, clearing his throat as he pulled his hat down over his head.

He said, "I have to go there."

§

Local strangers passed us on the street, faces turned to a cloudy sky as they wondered would it be another day of in-and-out showers or if maybe the sun would make another go of it after all. Some passed in a perpetual embrace, cuddling and rubbing Eskimo kisses, others laughing as they waved away a joke. After enough of their smiling faces, I slipped the quarter-on-a-hay-string from around my neck, dropping it down a drain.

We soon passed the Herring House and were approaching Ernul's when Spike slowed, wandering absently to the old alley next to the bar. I stopped and waited, pulling a smoke from my pack and staring at thunderheads building in the distance, forming a ghost-like pall over the town.

But Spike just kept sort of strolling around in the alley there, back and forth, and I was about to ask him what the hell he thought he was doing when all at once he came smiling back over.

"You know what, Wes? Actually, I think there's somewhere I gotta be..."

I looked at him then, at the furtive knowledge dancing like a dervish in his eyes but forever veiled beyond the mask of his thick, over-sized lenses. Or was that only my imagination? Before I could decide, he reached inside his jacket and pulled something out, handing it over.

"Do me a favor...give this to Prentice for me, will ya?"

Taking it in my hands, I saw it was the book Aunt Joyce had given me all those weeks ago, and that I in turn had given Spike to give to Prentice. I couldn't imagine what sorts of things were written inside those pages, and wasn't about to find out.

Spike gave me a playful jab on the shoulder and then turned, strolling away past Ernul's and down Oyster Boulevard, vanishing around the corner of Darlington Road. Then I was alone and staring at the book, turning it in my hands.

Paths to God, it was called.

§

When I got there, the barn was deserted.

Instruments shone brightly on the stage across the room, reflecting what little sun was left in the sky, and stepping inside I noticed the word CYA-NIDE scrawled in bright puce-colored paint along the back wall.

I found Prentice in his room. Not collapsed in a corner but head hung low near an old kerosene heater, face obscured by a stringy mop of hair as I stepped inside and just sort of stood there against the wall, waiting for him say something, anything at all. He didn't, and finally I stumbled over, lighting another smoke and lowering myself next to him on the floor.

My knees were starting to hurt.

never saw Ray again after that night. Not in any real way, at least, and definitely not in any way worth remembering.

Reprinted from the Reelsboro *Sun Journal*, dated September 22, 1987:

ARAPAHOE—The body of a man found near the tracks of the Norfolk Southern Railway system on Sunday has been identified as Honore Eugene Lafargue, 36, of Abbeville, Louisiana. Lafargue was first spotted sometime after eight o'clock Monday morning by Bud Tarkington, an engineer for the NS Railway. "At first I thought it was a dead animal," says Tarkington, "you know, maybe a deer, something like that. It was early, and the fog was still kind of high. Then I seen the face, and I knew it was a lot uglier than that."

The discovery sent shockwaves throughout the small coastal community. Lafargue had sustained severe third-degree burns covering his body, though the exact cause of death remains uncertain. The Reelsboro County Sherriff's Department has made no arrests in connection with the case, though Deputy Michael Lunsmann says foul play has "definitely not been ruled out."

Lafargue, known as "Ray" to his friends, had been staying in the Reelsboro area for several months at the time of his death. A lifelong fisherman, he was familiar to many residents...

Two days after the story ran, Keri Scott appeared on my porch. She'd been crying, I could tell, and for a second there I wasn't sure if maybe she'd swing on me. Instead, she said, "What ain't you telling me that I need to know?" She was sort of breathing hard, staring back at me in that silly-serious sort of way that people do. "*Tell me, Weston Mercer...*"

I, for one, wondered how much she already knew. I searched her deep brown eyes, the puffy mourning of her face, but in the end decided there was just no way to tell. So I lied.

I hear she still lives out there, probably in that same trailer, probably working that same job under that same fat-nosed manager. Probably looking old as all get-out.

I know I do.

Yes, and that's to be expected, I suppose, for thirty years ago I was a much younger man; not quite a teenager, but no less impulsive, no less ignorant. I've grown a lot since then, and seen things no man should ever have to see, learned a lot of things we as rational members of the human race have no reason learning. I've learned, for instance, that sometimes life has a way of putting your face in the mud, of sticking it there and then holding it, and in those times you have either one of two options: breathe in the brown stuff or stop breathing at all. And as for me...well, I'm still breathing, believe it or not. I've learned that sometimes life has a way of becoming something *other* than life, something not life at all but actually much darker—something we don't much like looking at but find, in our deepest of dreams, we can't escape.

And I believe it was precisely these sorts of things that made Prentice what he was in those days—or that made him necessary at all: in the end, no more than a figure on which to hang our own drunken lust and fury and addiction; something tangible, that could be smelled and touched and tasted. A self-fulfilling idol to be set up on those long weekend nights.

Prentice accepted the role—and relished it, I

think. But had it not been him, it would've been somebody else; there were always others, of course. Always will be. And in desperate times, when that senseless rage comes eating at our hearts and our fists shake for want of some warm hand to hold them, any old schlock rocker will do—as long as he doesn't break face, doesn't allow us to look into the mirror and see ourselves not there. As long as he's a convincing enough reflection of us all. And, of course, he must never look back in anger; must never puff up at the laity, and insult too greatly the ones who made him.

Prentice had done this.

And yet apart from this one item, he'd been the best...the best, that is, until the life became too much for him. Maybe he'd relished it a little *too* much and that's why it could never last, could never be something stable but was so much like Prentice himself, always on the verge of exploding in a ball of flashing white fire.

We buried him last week. Not from an overdose, or another night of Tvarscki-induced terror, or some capricious drug deal gone wrong. No, none of that at all. That Friday night show of September '87 was the last Olympus ever performed; the next week Prentice moved back home, and later that following year I followed suit. Spike, meanwhile, inherited Ray's treasured dredger from Stick Folsom (something Ray hadn't told us: the dredger had been paid in full for over three weeks at the time of his death).

After a couple years at the Weyerhouser plant, Prentice went to work for Man's End, some big-deal recovery program out of Nashville. Then last year he fulfilled what he saw as his true calling in life, joining some famous book-club gig called Gideons International. Seven months later, Prentice Cerona left on what would've been his first overseas trip with the group...only his flight never arrived. It was the US Airways flight out of Charlotte; you might have read about it in the papers. Search parties were called off after the second week.

The plane was never found.

Spike and I stood side by side at the service, him with his wife and couple of kids, me alone. It would've been the first time the three of us had been together in over four years, had Prentice been there. Had there been anything to put in the coffin besides the old Harmony acoustic he was still apt to play on those long rides or during quiet times in whatever place he was in. Or letters from all the people whose lives he'd touched, in one way or another, through the years. But he wasn't.

He wasn't there.

And as they'd readied to lower this bodiless trunk once and for all, my mind began to wander, as it is apt to do this time of year. As it happened, today it was wandering to Shakes, a brutish, slack-jawed beast of a man I'd first met during my prison days. He'd always reminded me of Prentice, in a way, despite being much too old for the part (and had as many wrinkles to prove it). Really it was in the eyes, I think, and the way everything seemed somehow more exciting when he talked about them. And remembering Shakes led me to thinking about the grimy prison bars themselves, and the couple healthy spoonfuls of brown sugar that had put me behind them.

I tried straightening up my act a little after getting out, and did a fairly decent job of it, too. That was nine years ago though—The Parole Years—and now I'm truly free, no probation, no parole. Finally able to vote again, but still can't own a firearm. Seriously, though, what do I need with a gun?

Oh yeah, and since he's back in town for the funeral, Spike is having some sort of tent revival meeting next week (he's out of the fish business these days, and has turned his attention to, what did the flyer call it—*small community faith rallies?* Whatever that means). I suppose I'll stop by. It bothers me sometimes, hearing that stuff, but I can stick it out, I guess, for Spike's sake: our last huzzah before we go our separate ways for the next oh, who knows how many years. Maybe for the last time.

Never know.

Besides, it'll never be like it was with us before, especially now that Prentice is gone. But even if he wasn't it'd still never be the same, not if I know those two like I think I do. Sometimes I wonder what happened to those guys, but then my mind starts going places I don't particularly like it to go and I just have to settle for the fact that those days—days of siphoning the pockets of some rich mummy's Benz, or cruising Ernul's for a good buzz before the show and watching a red-clad Eddie Murphy cut it up for no one but us—well, those days are dead...and never coming back.

And yet still on those long nights, when sleep comes hard or not at all, occasionally my thoughts wander to the farthest shores and I see a dark fortress leading higher and higher through a mist. And sometimes I wonder, had I time to search this great labyrinth of horrors, how long it might take to find *my* cell, my own drowned spirit only waiting to be consumed by the death and sorrow of that place? I see sunken faces peering through the darkness, their cracked hands reaching out, out, out. Or maybe it's Ray that I see, eyes peering up and up and up as he stands bathed in the brilliance of some ethereal firefly from above...

But most of all I think back to a time when I was much younger, and things made much more sense. I think back to the first time the three of us had ever been together, gathered in the ruins of my once-future living room, Prentice strumming wildly at a broken guitar. Spike speaking stoically the words to an old Kenny Rogers classic. And me, wondering just what I had gotten myself into, moving to a backwards, edge-of-nowhere place like Reelsboro County.

ABOUT THE AUTHOR

Hamelin Bird is the author of *Double Vision*, which *Publishers Weekly* called "a creepy, nightmarish debut" and was a 2021 Da Vinci Eye Award Finalist. He lives and works in North Carolina.

www.hamelinbird.com